THE GOD'S WOLFLING
(CHILDREN OF MYTH, #2)

THE CHILDREN OF MYTH

CEDAR SANDERSON

SANDERLEY STUDIOS

Cedar Sanderson
Originally Published by Stonycroft Publishing
Second Edition by Sanderley Studios

Cover Design by Cedar Sanderson
Editing by Jason Dyck

✿ Created with Vellum

Dedicated to my children, who inspire me and give me the impetus to keep going onward and upward. Gladiana, Juliet, Philippa, and Johann, you are the magic in my life.

ACKNOWLEDGMENTS

Many thanks, as well, to my beta readers who helped make this story all it could be. After the time elapsed between the first one and this finale, I wasn't sure... you all helped a bunch.

PROLOGUE

*N*othing lasts forever. The beings who designed this system had known that, so they opted for double back-ups and redundant wiring. What they had not anticipated was that memories fail. Even theirs. Long before humanity was self-aware, the memories had started to slip, to become erroneous. The back-up systems needed maintenance, once a millennium or so, but no-one in this reality knew that. Perhaps not even in the Other plane, the one the beings had come from.

Contact from their home had been lost for so long that those who were called gods, spirits, immortals became tired, forgetful, and – mostly – lost. Some few of them had retreated to this place, whose origin and intention had been forgotten, to sleep for eternity. They believed they could not die; their ability to do so had been forgotten, just as this prison had been misremembered as an asylum from the madness that ran amok on Earth. Blood-spattered, they reached it and sighed with relief, helping one another find rest, or so they thought. Dreamless sleep had claimed them for centuries, and the machines that held them suspended hummed on.

The corrosion would have been familiar to any human technician's eye by the time the machine failed. A grayish-white oxide that eroded through wires at a rate of years for each molecule lost, a rate slower than the tech might have understood, but then, when the beings had lain down, that human would have gaped and mumbled magic at the sight of stasis tanks. Now, here, while the wires were cracking, that man would have at least been able to guess at what they were, and possibly even reverse-engineer them, if not completely understand what they did.

The being in the failing tank began to awaken. He lifted a trembling hand to his brow, brushing rime-frost from his bushy eyebrows, and then looked at it in confusion.

"It's in the water." His voice was more a rusty rumble, possibly not even understandable had anyone been listening. He tried to sit up.

It took him a few tries to get out of the stasis box. Far above the chamber, the sun rose and set over a desolate Icelandic landscape. Finally, he was able to stagger to the box that held his beloved. He could see her, *there*, covered in frost and utterly still, but he could not reach her. He clawed at the cover for a release, screaming in frustration and rage when he could not find one. Eventually he collapsed on the floor next to her, half sobbing, his hand caressing the box and leaving bloody streaks from his broken fingernails.

He slept while the sun rose and set in another day on this accursed planet. When he awakened, he remembered. He caressed her coffin one last time, and strode away, his shoulders set in determination.

The sun was rising again when he emerged, and he shivered in the thin, cutting wind. He cupped his hands and whispered into them while the sun threw shadows all around him, then flung his hands up and out, releasing the message-bird he had just created. With one last command, he gave it a direction.

"Hephaestus." Manannan Mac'Lir cried aloud. "Find the Smith!"

1

BOREDOM

*L*inn tried to uncross her eyes for about the hundredth time. Hypatia was a dear, a font of wisdom, but when she got going on a pet topic, Linn could feel her eyes glaze over. She couldn't just make an excuse and get away; she had to sit and listen, since Hypatia was now officially her primary teacher.

Pele and Theta had announced that she would not attend public school on the Big Island. Too dangerous, it had been decided. It was a small island, and an even smaller community, and there would be curiosity. Having grandparents who were gods of ancient times, and a mother who was also fully immortal was cool, but had unforeseen consequences. So, Linn had lessons with Daffyd, and Hypatia, and sometimes others who travelled in and out of Sanctuary. It was much easier than public school, she had to admit, and she learned more than her former school could have taught her. Being taught by the former librarian of the Library of Alexandria was a definite plus.

It wasn't as though she didn't have friends. Bes, the dwarf Egyptian god, made a point of dropping by and teaching her self-defense and what he called 'cunning classes.' Deirdre shared lessons along with Linn, although today she was working, and her cousins took part in some classes. Deirdre was a coblyn, with green skin and long pointed ears, and a very geek mind in between them. All the coblyns were related, Linn had discovered, although some so distant it left her hopelessly confused.

It was just that she wished she were more useful. But ever since the battle on the High Plane, and the installation of the EMP weapon, it seemed to her that the war had gone cold. She wanted it resolved. Heff disappeared on mysterious missions from time to time, and she knew that had to be about the elder gods and the conflict, but he wouldn't talk about it. She was equally certain that had anything major happened it would have been all over Sanctuary about a minute later.

Linn knew that she was only sixteen, so she couldn't do a lot, yet, even though a hundred years ago – or even back in the time of the gods! – she would have been a full-grown adult. Hypatia stopped talking. Linn jumped guiltily, aware that she had not been paying attention.

"Yes?" She ventured, wondering if she had missed a question.

"Do you need a recess?" Hypatia's smile took the sting out of having been caught daydreaming.

"I'm sorry." Linn really did feel bad about it. "I'm just... distracted."

Hypatia came and sat down at the table next to her. "Want to talk about it?"

"I don't know," Linn responded. "I guess I just feel useless."

"You want some more adventures?"

"Yeah. Summer before last was exciting in bad ways at times, but I had a purpose. I needed to get the kittens here, and then Bes..." Her voice trailed off as she remembered his terrible wounds.

"But now, nothing happens?"

Linn could hear the laughter in Hypatia's voice, and she could see that she was being a little silly. She wasn't important, except as the daughter of Theta, a child of the gods. Children who had the power of the gods were rare, and guarded carefully.

"I know, that's a good thing," she admitted grudgingly.

Hypatia shook her head. "I know I am the very model of the cloistered scholar. But I do understand that experience is every bit as important as book learning. I'll talk to Pele, since Theta is traveling. You need some exercise, both physical and mental."

Linn couldn't get excited about this, but she said thank you. Hypatia shooed her out of her office.

"Take Blackie and go swimming," she said.

Linn made her escape. There wasn't a big surf at the Sanctuary beach, but she had been learning how to body-surf and it sounded a lot better than sitting in a windowless office. She stopped in the common room, looking for the big cats. No longer kittens, Blackie was easily the size of a Bengal tiger, and Spot not far behind him. The tabby was less heavily muscled, though, built like a cheetah. Unlike house cats, they both loved to swim.

They were sitting and attentively listening to Bes hold forth on something; battle, no doubt. Both boys were obsessed with war. Linn sometimes thought Blackie, at least, ought to know better.

This crossed her mind in an instant, then she bowled into their midst to hug Bes. She hadn't seen him in ages.

"Here now!" He held her out at arm's length to look at her. "You're no taller than you were, so how have you gotten bigger?"

Linn shook her head at him. "I've shrunk, just look at the boys."

She put her hand on Blackie's head, well above waist height on her. Spot, laughing, reared up and put his paws on her shoulders from behind, knocking her forward. Bes caught her with one hand and cuffed Spot behind the ear with the other.

"I think you need to burn off some energy, kitten."

"I was going to the beach," Linn extricated herself as Blackie used his shoulder to shove his brother out of the way.

"Sounds like a plan." Bes set her down and ruffled Spot's fur.

"Oh, good, you're coming with?" She followed the big cats at a distance, as they were now play-fighting their way along the corridor.

"Don't have anything better to do," he ambled alongside her with his bow-legged stroll.

She tried to sound casual. "The war has cooled down?"

"Yes and no," he surprised her by actually giving her an answer. It always seemed to Linn that the adults in her life sidestepped when she brought it up.

"There is no overt action, but little nasty incidents. Someone tried to get into Coyote's valley; we don't know who, or why, unfortunately. The Monster didn't leave us anything but ashes."

Linn frowned, "Why would they want to get in there?"

"Because his power is very great. He's older than... I don't know. Older than I am, but Coyote never gives a straight answer, you know."

"Crooked as a dog's hind leg," she murmured with a smile at her own joke.

"Ayup," he agreed with an evil grin.

They came out into the bright sunlight at the tunnel's end and headed for the bathhouse.

Pele kept it stocked with suits in all sizes, for Bes, and other visitors, and Linn had gotten in the habit of keeping hers in there after forgetting it in her room too many times. The big cats were already splashing in the surf. Linn could see there wasn't enough wave action for surfing, but she wasn't in the mood for that anyway. She wanted to talk to Bes.

It seemed odd to her, she mused, clipping her long hair up and out of her way for swimming, to be so comfortable when there was a war on. Sure, most of the human world had no idea, but she knew. The beach scene seemed like cheating with what she knew and had seen. She stepped out of the changing room into the sun and blinked.

Bes had beat her into the water. She noted with approval that he was letting his hair go as black as his skin again. She had pointed out to his that he had no real need to look old, and he certainly didn't act old. Unlike her grandfather.

Linn ran into the cool sea, throwing up a shower of sparkling drops shot through with rainbows, and scooped up a double-handful of water to fling at Bes. He retaliated, and she let her worries go in the laughing conflict of the moment. It ended with her lying breathless on her back at the very edge of the water. The waves lapping at her legs cooled them, but her cheeks burned from the heat of her exertions. It felt nice.

Bes dropped into lotus position by her head. Blackie and Spot came and stretched out into the dry sand nearby.

"Bes?" Linn began, feeling oddly shy.

"Pop out the question, kiddo, before you pop." He reached down and pulled a strand of wet hair out of her face. She arched her head back so she could see his face. He was smiling a little, and she felt the familiar tickle of irritation at adults anticipating her all the time, like nothing she said or did really surprised them.

"Am I old enough?" she asked finally.

He tipped his head slightly to one side. Linn sighed, and went on, "ok, maybe that was too vague."

He shook his head. "I think I got it. You are ready to leave the safe place and do something with all that boundless energy. Why have power, and not use it?"

"I want to be useful. I feel like all I am doing here is staying out of the way."

"In all my centuries, I've seen a lot of war. And more peace. Teenager is a new concept, you know. It wasn't that long ago when a girl your age was married. A boy your age was working hard to support his family, and you'd be working right alongside him," he stopped to take a deep breath. "It's better, now. You get a chance to grow up, to really learn something, before you have to focus on raising a family of your own."

Linn sat up. "I don't want a family. I don't even want a boyfriend."

He laughed. "Good, otherwise Heff and I would have to go talk to him."

She laughed along with him at the thought of some poor boy having to stand up to the two of them in full parental mode.

"You're champing at the bit. Nothing wrong with that. You're old enough to start working and test yourself." He reached out and tapped her on the nose. "Just don't go looking for trouble?"

Linn nodded. She had no intention of finding trouble, she just wanted to do something. Her stomach rumbled audibly, making them both laugh again.

"How about lunch?" Bes suggested, just before being bowled over by three teens headed for food.

2

RELAXATION

*H*alfway around the planet from the newly-awakened god and his plight, Heff Vulkane, once known as the Smith of the Gods, set his fruity drink down on the little table at his elbow and stretched his toes in the black volcanic sand, sighing with contentment. He was enjoying a rare vacation, something he was rediscovering made hard work worthwhile. During the decades of his self-imposed retirement and hermitage in the mountains of Idaho, he had done very little. Now, as one of the leaders in the private war to keep Earth free, he had very little free time.

To make his enjoyment complete, Pele walked out of the waves in front of him, crystal drops of water catching the sunlight, and his breath. She came and leaned over him for a kiss, and he didn't mind the drips she shed as she took her time. She had given up Crone for Maiden, and was the curvy raven-haired beauty he had fallen for all those centuries before. When they came up for breath, a cleared throat off to their side made Heff chuckle.

"Deal, Kiddo. Your generation didn't invent sex." He informed his only grandchild.

"Yeah, Grandpa, I know." Linn gave him the hairy eyeball, and now

Pele laughed, sitting on the arm of his lounger and wringing her hair out into the sand so she wouldn't drip more on him.

"What's up?" He prompted the young woman who looked more and more like her grandmother with each passing year.

"I was hoping to talk to you about something."

Heff smiled at her and waved at the other chair. Pele stayed where she was. Heff studied his granddaughter for a long moment.

"You've grown," he mused.

She looked surprised, asking "since when?"

"Since you came here, dear." Pele filled in.

Linn shook her head. "I'm still as short as I was then."

"That's not what I meant. You are two years older, and it shows."

"The summer vacation from hell made me grow up, and since then, nothing has happened." Linn complained.

Heff nodded. "I thought that was what you were going to say."

Pele interjected her comment before Linn could respond. "You're bored. You've been stuck here with Hypatia, and you love her, and have learned about so many things, but when is the war going to end. Or begin? Or something?"

Linn threw her hands in the air with a short laugh and leaned back in her chair, unconsciously imitating her grandfather's earlier action by digging her toes into the sand.

"Yes! I helped create a weapon. Maybe. We don't know if it would actually work, since we never used it. I was running for my life. And then... it just stopped."

"Not completely." Heff sighed, thinking of all the nasty little skirmishes he'd been fighting for the last few years.

"You want to be part of it." Pele supplied.

"I guess. I mean, I know, it's dangerous for me. More than for you, or Bes. Who was here earlier today, by the way."

They nodded. Linn assumed her grandmother knew when anyone went through Sanctuary. Not the whole islands, her family wasn't that kind of god, to be omniscient, but Pele kept a close eye on the comings and goings here.

"And I know I can't fight, don't want to..." she stopped, stuck for words.

"What about Patches and Moira?" Pele asked.

Linn shrugged. "They are doing preschool. Sometimes I play with them on the beach, but they're babies."

Her grandparents exchanged amused looks, and Linn went on with her train of thought. "Deirdre, Blackie, and Spot are good friends, but it's not like school in Seattle was, with all my friends there. I miss some, and not others. Sanctuary is wonderful, Hypatia is an amazing teacher, she knows so much. It's just..." she trailed off, her train derailed by what she was seeing.

She was looking past them, toward the cliff-face of Sanctuary, when she saw Sekhmet emerge from the tunnel at a lope, only transforming to woman-form as she neared them. Linn had never seen her do this before, and she stared, transfixed.

Heff and Pele, seeing her expression, turned in their chairs to see who or what was coming. Sekhmet had already finished her shift, which Linn had seen as a golden flowing of Power and fur, finishing in the goddess's golden-skinned woman-form. She was dressed, too, in the pleated white cotton dress of Ancient Egypt.

Sekhmet winked at Linn, who was stunned speechless, and held out her hands to Pele, who rose to give her a hug.

"I thought you were on vacation," Heff hugged his right-hand woman in turn.

"Oh, you know how that goes." The lion goddess stooped to kiss her sons, then held out her arms to Linn. Sekhmet smelled faintly spicy, and she rested a cheek on Linn's hair in a rare moment of stillness. The big cat was more industrious than any tame tabby.

"I need to talk to Heff and Pele, brave girl." Sekhmet murmured to Linn. Still in her arms, Linn could hear her heart pounding. She resented being treated like a child, but something that frightened Sekhmet was a scary thought.

"Go ahead, Sek. Linn can hear this: she's going to go to work for us," Grandpa Heff said.

Linn bounced out of Sekhmet's grasp, excited. "Really?"

Pele laughed. "First job: settle and listen."

Linn plopped down on the sand cross-legged and put a hand on her chin, fingers over her mouth.

"Ok," Sekhmet laughed, "new recruit is inducted."

She stood with her arms clasped behind her back and her face dropping into seriousness. Linn could feel a tingle as the Power surged through Sekhmet. The tall woman was gathering herself.

"Steve took me to the Grand Canyon, his idea of being funny. I hadn't been there – one of the few places I haven't visited-" she began.

Grandpa Heff interrupted her quietly. "Get to it. No easier for delay."

"Ran into Coyote." Sekhmet cut right to the point.

"Ran into? More like he intercepted you." Pele interrupted with a sniff. "He never does anything by accident. Sorry, we keep interrupting you. I'll imitate Linn now." She propped her elbows on her knees and put her chin on her hands, covering her mouth and smiling at her granddaughter.

Sekhmet chuckled; her tension broken. "Oh, I know. He was pretty transparent, just strolled out of the canyon we were hiking past. But what he wanted was to get a message to you."

Linn blurted out, "why doesn't he come himself?" She felt her cheeks burn as all three adults looked at her.

"Good question," Heff grunted.

"He said he couldn't leave the area, he's keeping an eye on it, that he'd come too far already just for a visit with Steve and I."

"He's using too much power to look through animal eyes, he can't get too far from his network," Pele interjected, looking at Linn, who nodded that she understood.

She had learned that technique, pinching off a little Power and letting it go into an animal and hitch a ride. It was tiring for her, but she was only a demi-god.

Sekhmet went on. "He said to tell you the game is afoot in the Great Caldera."

"Oh. Pele, where is Theta right now?"

"Iceland. She went to the lamia's grave." Pele and Sekhmet both looked sad. Linn wondered what that was about.

"We have to go." Pele's voice was as firm as Linn had ever heard her.

"Steve went to Quetzalcoatl with the message, and I came to you."
Now, Sekhmet just sounded tired.

"Good." Heff nodded. "That will speed things along. If Coyote is worried, something is in the wind."

As he said wind, a little bird dropped out of the air into his lap. Heff jumped.

The tiny brown plover looked dead at first, and Linn stood up, wondering what had happened to it. Heff scooped it into his palms and lifted it to his face, blowing on it. Linn could see a little spark of Power go into it. Gradually, it righted itself, looking around with beady eyes, but it didn't fly away.

"Speak," Heff commanded it gruffly.

It opened its mouth—beak, bill? Linn wasn't sure—and a man's voice sounded loudly. "Hephaestus, Smith, Artificer, I beseech thee for assistance. I, Manannan Mac'Lir, call upon the bonds of the sea, through which we are brothers, to draw thee to me. I await thee in my home, heart lain low until thy succor is at hand."

Linn looked at the adults, confused. She had never seen this kind of thing, a sort of bird voice mail, she supposed, and not too hard with Power. But who was Manannan Mac'Lir?

"I need to find Bes. Is he still here?" Heff looked at Linn and Pele. Both nodded, and Heff headed for the tunnel entrance to Sanctuary, still holding the bird.

Pele looked at Linn and Sekhmet and sighed. "Shall we go pack for me to leave, since the men are off chasing wild birds?"

This made them all laugh, and Linn followed them into the rooms her grandparents shared, a rather book-cluttered suite in a quiet corner of the refuge Pele had carved – literally – out of the heart of a mountain. She helped pack a suitcase, wondering how on earth her grandmother planned to carry it, and then watched with wide eyes as the bag was made to vanish.

"Where..." she asked in confusion, looking around the room.

"It's sort of... inter-dimensional." Sekhmet explained. "You know how the High Plane and the Low, or Earth, works, right?"

"Parallel universes, right?"

"Simply put, yes. The High Plane actually isn't higher than Earth, it's just what we named it when we learned how to access it, with a little jump upwards and a boost of Power."

Linn nodded. She could do that herself, now, although for long trips she would need someone with more Power to help. "There are at least three, that you- we," she corrected herself, "know of, and we can only access two."

Pele nodded. "Most of us have lost all memory of the third plane, our homeworld, except as dreamy, magical memories. Anyway, my bag is right there." She pushed a hand upward over her head, and it disappeared for a second, eerily, and then she pulled the case halfway into reality to show Linn before restoring it to the other, unseen dimension. "I can access it whenever and wherever I want it. Saves a lot of effort.

"Now that's done, I want to gather up Heff and get going. Don't think I can't see you itching to get out of here." Pele addressed the other goddess.

Sekhmet was sitting, but had she been in cat form her tail would have been twitching violently. She sighed. "I wish I could say I didn't have a very bad feeling."

"What's the Great Caldera?" Linn ventured, as they headed for the common area.

"Oh... I think your mother could answer that best."

"Cell phones don't exactly work in Sanctuary." Linn replied dryly.

"Look up the Yellowstone Volcanic Caldera, dear." Her grandmother told her as they reached the big room, not looking at Linn, but for Heff. "Consider it homework. There they are."

Linn pulled out her phone and made a note of it. She didn't have cell service, but it made a decent personal organizer anyway. She was looking down and following Pele and Sekhmet with her peripheral vision, weaving through chairs and couches.

"Ah, there you are." Her grandfather got out of the chair he'd been sitting in, leaning forward to talk intently to Bes. "Linn, find out what Manannan needs. I'm sending you, Blackie, and Spot along with Bes. Think of it as a training mission."

Bes, slouched comfortably on a couch, smirked. "That means there will be rain. It's not good training unless there is rain."

Heff shot him a look. "Yes, there will likely be rain. He's probably on the Isle of Man."

Linn, standing in front of her grandfather now, shifted her stance to relax a little. She could feel the adrenaline crackling like lightning in her veins. She was going to get out and do something. Even if it was training, that was a good start.

The little bespelled bird hopped off her grandfather's finger and chirruped, cocking his head slightly and fixing a beady eye on Linn. She smiled. He was a cute little puffball of feathers, and the contrast of his softness next to her grandfather's callused, scarred palm struck her as ironic. He fluttered into the air suddenly, startling her.

Bes laughed and the little bird came and perched on his bushy hair. He held up a hand and coaxed it down. "We will take you home, little one." He promised it gravely.

"How did something so tiny make such a long flight?" Linn wondered aloud.

"Use your sight," Heff suggested.

"Ok..." she squinted carefully at the bird. "Oh, it's a bit of Power..." the shifting aura was a gray-green, the color of a stormy sea. She had realized that Power signatures were somehow related to the affinity of the god that generated them. Heff's was red as fire, for instance. Her own attenuated power signature was pink.

Heff nodded. "Another reason to return him, so Manannan can reabsorb that. He was never the strongest of us, but cunning."

Lin was reminded of a fragment of power she had in keeping for him and asked, "Should I take Lambent?"

Bes nodded. "Always armed."

"Pack light, though. You ought to be back within a week." Her grandfather instructed.

"Why are we going, again?" she asked.

He raised an eyebrow, "I have to go to Yellowstone."

Linn could feel herself blush, "No, I meant why not just send messages."

"Ah. Bes, you get to explain Manannan to her," Heff held out his arms for a hug. "I have to run."

Linn leaned into his barrel chest, soaking up his warmth and inhaling his faintly smoky smell. He always smelled like that, even when he hadn't been near his forge, that she knew of, in weeks. Her grandmother always smelled of frangipani. Linn let go, and he was out the door, leaving her looking at Bes. Sekhmet and her grandmother had gone already.

He wiggled his eyebrows at her and made a ridiculous face. "Ready for an adventure?"

"I'm not sure I want adventure. I just wanted to be helpful."

He stood up, and the little bird went back to his hair. "Everything is an adventure. Now, go pack. And seriously, bring rain gear."

She went. She was excited: this really was going to be an adventure, even if all they did was play courier. Blackie and Spot were waiting in the common area when she came back in with her backpack, and she joined them, looking around for Bes. Deirdre made a beeline for her.

"Hey, guess what?"

Linn smiled down at her friend. "What?"

"I get to come along!" The tiny greenish teenager bounced in her excitement.

"It's Bes' traveling school and circus," that god broke in with an amused chuckle. He addressed Linn's best friend. "Deirdre, do you have your gear?"

She nodded, her long pointy ears flopping a little with the force of her enthusiasm. Her fine brown hair, cut short, made her look like a pixie rather than the proto-goblin that she was.

The coblyns that inhabited the Sanctuary as the main colony and administrators (not to mention builders), were not surly tricksters. Linn had learned that Deirdre's grandfather was their king, a rather laissez-faire ruler who left the actual work to his management team. When they had left Britain centuries before, the clans who chose to remain had become the goblins of legend and lore. Linn realized that she didn't know much about their history, really. Maybe this trip would be a good time to ask Deirdre about it.

Linn slung her backpack on her shoulders, thinking that she really needed to learn Pele's trick, which would be less work. She held out her hands, one for Bes, and the other for Deirdre. It was much easier to get on the High Path, and stay together, if they were in contact. The big cats disdained this, leaping with them as they set off, and becoming ghostly shadow cats once they were in the tunneling space of the inter-dimensional highway. The human forms ran lightly, paced by the cats on each flank of their group.

Linn realized she hadn't even had time to properly research the Isle of Man, let alone ask Bes about Manannan Mac'Lir. She did so now, and he responded without breaking stride. He was being slow for them, she knew.

"He's a sea god, and a trickster, like Coyote, or me. He's been... asleep for a long time. Which is why the archaic message and speech when he summoned your grandpa."

"And why we need to go to him in person?"

"Yes, it's a gesture of respect and also lets us check him out."

"For what?"

"Well, some of the Elder gods are not quite right, anymore."

Linn snorted. "So, we're walking into the house of a crazy guy?"

"Castle," he corrected, "and yes, but Manannan has always been crazy. Heff just needs to know how crazy. You guys are safe, though," he assured her, looking at her face and seeing the worry Linn knew she was showing. "Kids are sacred to Manannan. You'll see."

3

TRAVEL

*T*he High Path always fascinated Linn. It wasn't strictly speaking a path at all, and it didn't go anywhere. The first time she had walked it, with Blackie's help, she had been too scared and worried to pay much attention, and there had been very few opportunities to examine it closely since that wild night when she and Blackie had saved Bes's life as he lay helpless on the battlefield.

Now she looked at the 'walls' as they walked. Blackie kept pace with her, and they were a little ahead of the others. The High Path, Linn knew, was an extra-dimensional tunnel through the space between universes. Earth was only one of at least three universes, Linn knew for sure. The others were the long-lost world the gods and spirits of myth had fallen from untold years before, and the world they used as a rest place. Only those who carried the nano-machines which made 'magic' possible could use the High Path, and cross between the worlds. Linn, by virtue of the ones she had inherited from her mother, could travel on it, but she needed help to make that first step, still.

She was fairly sure that if she stopped moving, the High Path would still take her where she was meant to go, but she had been cautioned not to stop while on the path. She'd been studying quantum mechanics, just the basics, and was puzzling over how that related to this gray, shimmery stuff that didn't look, or... she reached out and poked the wall cautiously. It didn't feel like much, but sort of deformed away from her hand, leaving a bit of a pocket in the smooth wall.

Blackie made a noise and batted at her leg with his big paw.

"Oops." Linn realized she had stopped walking and started up again. Then she stopped, making the big kitten yowl as she stepped on his toe. "Where are the others?"

He looked behind them along with her. It was sort of foggy, and she couldn't see or hear anything. Maybe they had walked past while she was checking the wall out. Linn shrugged and started to walk quickly, giving up on the strange other-worldly substance.

"Bes? Deirdre?" Linn called out. Her voice was just sort of swallowed up. There were no echoes, nor sense of distance. No answering call came out of the foggy tunnel. Linn bit her lip, wondering how far ahead they were, and kicking herself mentally for being so scatter-brained. She really couldn't do that, and this was undoubtedly Bes's way of teaching her not to lose track of her surroundings.

Linn sighed, and kept going. From what she understood of how the High Path worked, they would all come out at the same place, and she wouldn't stop and get separated from her party again on it.

"Okay, Bes." She called out, not expecting an answer. "I learned my lesson. See you when we get there!"

4

MESSENGER

*L*inn stopped at the edge of the high path, studying it intently. The transition between worlds shimmered, a little, and she knew from experience it would be like stepping through the looking glass into a whole 'nother place, from the gray tunnel of the Path. This metaphor amused her, and she giggled. Blackie butted her thigh with his head, knocking her sideways a step.

"Oof!" she regained her balance. "You're getting too big for kitten tricks, mister. And yes, I'm nervous, doing this alone. I wish Bes and Deirdre hadn't gone ahead. "

That they had gotten separated at all put her on edge. Setting out together on the High Path usually meant you wound up in the same place. When Linn had lost track of them, she wasn't sure. Probably when she had stopped and been daydreaming. Linn was afraid they hadn't come to right place even now. She did know it was time to take the next step, and be fully part of the adult's world. She was tired of being treated as a child.

These last two years there had been a lot of interrupted conversations when she or the other young ones were around, and mysterious comings and goings. Which left her and Blackie on this errand, to take Grandpa Heff's apologies to his old friend... although the look on Grandpa's face when he'd said that made Linn wonder how friendly it really was. If she had learned one thing in these illuminating years, it was that odd alliances had been forged over the millennia of the shadowy myth wars.

Quetzalcoatl, Sekhmet and Bes, Coyote... although Coyote, she understood, was a wild card. No one ever knew when or where he would pop up. And her grandfather, the only Olympian amongst them, and the de-facto war leader. Quetzalcoatl seemed to be the overall leader, but there was a loose council of sorts which would gather from time to time and make decisions. Linn knew they tried to stay out of human affairs as much as possible.

Two years ago, when she had arrived at Grandpa Heff's farm looking forward to summer vacation, she expected the biggest surprise to be the litter of kittens in the hayloft. She certainly didn't expect to find out her mother was the child of two gods, making Linn herself a demi-god. To learn this one night, and be on the run with the kittens practically the next moment had been an education in itself, and there had been a lot more to the summer after that.

Now, she squared her shoulders and stepped through the veil between worlds, from the High Path inter-dimensional corridor, back onto Earth, a half-globe away from where she had started that morning. It was raining a little, and very, very green. Even the birds were silent, and she could hear the sighing of ocean surf - very familiar after the last two years at Sanctuary in Hawaii - not too far off. But for now, they stood in deep forest.

Blackie lifted his nose, his mouth half-open. She recognized that he was using his Jacobsen's organ to smell the air deeply, detecting anything nearby. She couldn't hear anything but the raindrops pattering on leaves far overhead in the grove of trees. Maybe oaks? She wasn't sure. The big cat closed his mouth and then licked his nose.

"We're all alone, I think. Now how to find him?"

Linn turned in a circle, looking for a path, or a clue. It was hard to tell what time it was, or what direction north would be in, with the overcast hiding the sun. She'd been taught that when lost, to hug a tree and wait for help, but that didn't apply today. For one thing, she and Blackie could get on the High Path and head for home at any time. But that would mean admitting defeat. She picked a general direction.

"We go this way." Linn decided that if they could reach the ocean, they might be able to see better. And that was the other thing she knew. Find running water, follow it downward, and you would find civilization sooner or later. Here, she felt, it would be sooner. The Isle of Man wasn't that big, and had a lot of people in a relatively small area, as far as she was concerned. Blackie loped ahead of her, a rippling shadow under the trees.

The wet didn't bother her: it wasn't cold, and she had her raincoat. She knew it would be bad if she stayed out in it for too long, but she was confident that they would find shelter soon. Grandpa Heff had sent them here, and he wouldn't have let them come out too far from their destination. Training, on the other hand, happened best in the rain. She thought she detected Bes's hand in this imprecise targeting. She could hear his laughing voice in her head. "A good lesson, and a long walk, never hurt anyone."

The little Egyptian god had a wicked sense of humor, and had been her de-facto guardian that summer, and a friend as well as a teacher afterward. Linn missed him, but also wanted to prove that she'd been listening. She slicked her wet hair back off her face and paid attention. They were walking on a green carpet of mosses and grasses. It wasn't like the Pacific Rainforest she had grown up with outside of Seattle: it was firmer underfoot, and the trees were not as tall and broad. These trees gave off the impression of great age and character, she decided. They were gnarled and twisted overhead, with a directionality she recognized. They were coming close to the ocean, and the wind had sculpted the branches above over years of blowing in the same direction.

She couldn't feel the full force of the wind yet. Too many trees, still, and now there was low underbrush to push through, as well. She slowed down and made it carefully a bit further, losing sight of Blackie. Linn was pushing aside a branch to take another step when she felt a tug at her back.

"What?" Blackie tugged harder. Linn looked back at him, seeing that he had her coat in his mouth, his ears firmly flattened to his head. Mystified, she put her foot down rather than taking the next step, and tried to figure out what had him worried.

The brush was too thick to see through, here, so she pushed the branches aside in front of her again, and then realized why he had stopped her. There was a cliff on the other side of the bush she was trying to navigate through. Had she taken about two more steps, she would have fallen down it. Linn didn't dare get close enough to see how far down it went. Carefully, she retreated backwards through the bushes, Blackie keeping a tight hold on her coat until she was back into more open forest.

"Well." She wanted to sit down, but it was too wet. "Now what?"

It was getting darker, and she was hungry, thirsty, and quite put out. Bes and Deirdre still hadn't reappeared, which was beginning to worry her. She had water and food in her pack, of course, and she could have a drink, which she did now. Thinking, she munched a handful of GORP.

"Blackie, your turn. Obviously, my plan was for the birds."

He chuffed a snort at her, his version of a laugh. Swiveling his ears to and fro, he lashed his tail, hard, and then set out purposefully. Linn had to almost trot to keep up with him. With the light dimming, he was more shadowy than ever.

"I see now why you are superior camouflage cat." She told his tail. He twitched the tip of it in acknowledgement but didn't slow down. Linn saved her breath after that. He was in a hurry, and she was, too. Going home because it got dark would be very little-kid. They needed to find where they were, and what they were looking for. Most likely, Bes and Deirdre were already there.

It didn't take long at all, heading in this direction, to break out of the woods into an open, mowed field. Linn breathed a sigh of relief. She had been beginning to wonder if they had somehow ended up on the High Plane, in the vast wilderness areas. The rain was coming down harder, but perversely it seemed lighted now they were out from under the trees. Blackie semi-crouched in the muddy verge of the field, growling low in his throat.

"What's wrong?" She asked him. The big cat, unlike his mother, had never shifted to human form, but Linn had equally never doubted his personhood. She did, however, often wish he could or would talk. He laid his ears back, still growling, and his tail lashed.

Linn peered through the rain. "I think I see lights. Let's go."

The back of her neck was prickling with anxiety over the way Blackie was acting, and the idea of being somewhere warm, dry, and above all, lighted, sounded wonderful about now. That atavistic desire was the only thing she could think of, and it was why she stopped dead just before she opened the garden gate. She hadn't even thought about it, until this second, how normal people would react to her big black companion.

"Darn." As if on cue, another trickle of icy water made it past the collar of her coat and down her neck. "Blackie..." She really didn't want to leave him in the cold rain. He licked her hand and nudged her toward the gate. The he looked deliberately toward the barely visible bulk of the big barn. Linn sighed. He'd been born in a barn, after all, she just hated having to leave him out in the cold. He nudged her again, and she nodded and lifted the gate latch.

He'd vanished completely by the time she knocked at the heavy wooden door of the farmhouse. She was shivering in earnest now, and trying to pull together a coherent cover story to explain why she was out in the seeming middle of nowhere, lost and alone. Her knock seemed swallowed up in the dense wood of the door, like her voice had been by the High Path when she was calling Bes. Linn blinked back sudden tears, and knocked again.

The door opened with a suddenness that had her taking an involuntary step backwards, her hand still lifted up. Linn blinked at the apparition which had appeared before her. The goth chick with the piercings glared back from behind an unruly mop of obviously dyed black hair. Of everything Linn might have expected to find opening the door at a remote British farmhouse, this was the least plausible... She opened her mouth, finally, and managed, "H-hello?"

The creature scowled harder, and turned her... Linn could see now it was a girl perhaps her own age. She turned her head and bellowed in a piercing soprano, "Granda! Visitor!"

Linn stayed on the doorstep, not having been invited into the warm light that was spilling out around the figure of the girl in the NIN t-shirt and baggy black cargo pants. She could have stepped out of the halls of Linn's old school, which only made her that much more incongruous here. Footsteps sounded behind the girl, and she finally stepped aside. The man who came to the door was no taller than Linn, a half-head shorter than his own granddaughter, if Linn interpreted the appellation goth-chick had shouted correctly. His white hair stuck out from his head in what she suspected was a permanent halo of curls and wisps. He was drying his hands on a tattered dishtowel.

"Eh?" He peered at her, his blue eyes widening. "Child, you'll catch a death! Come, come..." Linn gratefully obeyed his beckoning hands and came dripping into the hall.

"Thank you." She got out around her chattering teeth.

"Here..." He pointed at the rack half-full of jackets, over a rack of boots. "Get oot o' t'wet."

Linn complied, feeling bad about the mess she was leaving on the worn stone flags of the floor. She hadn't realized quite how cold she was until she was fumbling with the laces of her muddy hiking boots. By the time she had them off, he was mopping the puddles she'd made up, expertly whisking it out the door with a flourish. Fascinated, she watched, wondering simultaneously how old he was, how old the house was, and just how many years it had taken of feet walking and bristly mops to wear the stone down like that. She glanced around and realized this place was old. Incredibly ancient, from the feel of it.

She couldn't risk a peek with her other sight, she needed to explain... "My name is..."

"Tsk. Coom, ha' tay."

Linn blinked, wondering what he had just said to her. She followed him into a little kitchen, where he sat her firmly at a chair drawn nearer the stove, which was open and had what looked like bricks of something burning in it. That, she thought, must be peat. She started to steam gently as the heat soaked into her damp clothing. He brought her a chipped mug full of a dark, hot beverage that smelled like... "Ah! Tea!" She smiled at him. He grinned back, a charmingly toothless smile that made him seem incredibly young and old all at once. He put a little plateful of cookies on the table near her elbow and turned back to his dishwater, leaving Linn to stare at his back, wondering where the goth apparition had gone, and why he wasn't curious about her.

"He's deaf as doornails." The goth-chick appeared in the doorway. "I'm Gloryann. Call me G."

Linn took the thin, pale hand, a little relieved that it was warm to the touch. "I'm Linn. I got separated from my group..."

"Ah, the lost." G made a face. "What inspires you yanks to walk in the rain."

"We, er, didn't have much time." Which was strictly true, even if Linn did hope G would take that as a short vacation, not an urgent mission.

"Better call them up, then. Let 'em know you aren't being eaten by ogres."

Linn blinked, and then realized she was being treated like a child and made fun of, not being given a serious warning. "Yes. Thank you for the tea and cookies."

G sniffed. "Biscuits. Crikies, didn't you watch Harry Potter, even?"

Linn nodded. "Sorry, I'm tired." She fumbled the cell phone out of the waterproof case her mother had insisted on, and when she looked up, G had gone again. Granda still stood at the sink washing, humming tunelessly.

She had one bar on the cell phone, and no idea if it would work overseas. With a helpless shrug, she dialed. To her delight, it not only went through, but Bes answered.

"Linn. Where are you? No, wait..." She could make out other voices in the background. "Never mind. I'm sending someone to pick you up. Sit tight until he arrives, Okay? And be careful what you say."

Then he hung up, leaving Linn staring at the phone in dismay. How did he even know where she was, when she didn't know herself? G drifted back into the room. "That was fast. He got a GPS tracker on you?"

Linn didn't know. That would be more reassuring than feeling like she had once again stumbled into something she didn't know enough about. "Where is... where are we?"

"You are lost, aren't you? We're near Ballentrae, just by Nickaloggie Burn."

Linn couldn't help it. She giggled at the name. G let her facade slip and cracked a smile. "Aye, it's not an easy name."

"This place seems... very old." Linn ventured, hoping the laugh hadn't offended the other girl.

G went back to her practiced gloom. "Old, rotten, and so boring I could die."

"Why are you here, then?" Linn had been wondering that since the goth had opened the door. G looked at her Granda's back. He'd moved from the finished dishes to a pan on the stove, which smelled appetizing to Linn's empty stomach.

"Not much choice."

She sat across the table from Linn, but didn't say anything more. Linn looked around the room. It was clean, but everything was worn. The curtains over the sink had been patched, carefully, but still. Linn couldn't help contrasting this place with her grandfather's cabin. They shared a certain homeyness, a warmth and comfort she could feel wrapping around her like a blanket. But the cabin was gone, blown to splinters by a vengeful god when her grandfather refused his overtures. Linn shivered a little.

G cocked her head suddenly. "I hear a car."

Linn stood up; certain this was her ride. The three of them went into the front hall, where Linn flinched from her clammy boots but resolutely forced her feet into them. Before shrugging into the wet coat, she held out her hand to Granda.

"Thank you." Linn pitched her voice a little high and enunciated clearly. He beamed at her again, revealing his gums in that baby-sweet smile.

"Welcome, child."

Linn turned to G as someone knocked at the door. "And thank you."

G ducked a shoulder gruffly and turned to the door. Instead of Bes, who Linn was expecting, a boy no older than she was stood there. He looked straight at her. "I was sent t' fetch you."

Linn hoped her mouth didn't drop open and show the dismay she felt. She had no idea who this was. Where were Bes, and Deirdre, and Spot? She thought for a fleeting second of appealing to G and the Granda, but they were nothing more than normal humans, who were to be kept out of conflicts at all costs. The slight accent of the boy meant he was likely a local, and thus linked to Manannan Mac'Lir... she stepped toward him, coat in hand.

"I'm ready. Goodbye." she said over her shoulder as she followed him down the path. Once the door was shut behind her, she hissed at him. "Who are you?"

"No time, get in the car," he pointed at the gate, where she could hear the engine still running. "I was told there were two of you?"

He looked around, and she went to the gate and let out a low whistle, then waited. He was just closing the gate when Blackie trotted out of the dark into the headlights, and Linn had the satisfaction of watching his jaw drop. She opened the passenger door, and the big cat flowed into the car, then she got in. Their chauffeur finally gathered his wits and climbed in his own door.

"I'm Merrick," he offered grudgingly.

"And I am Linnea, but I expect you knew that already?" She responded with a feeling of impatience. Where was Bes, and just who was this?

"I'm of Manannan Mac'Lir's Court. I was sent to fetch you."

Linn sighed and looked at his profile. He was paying close attention to the road, which she supposed she ought to be grateful for, as it was now pitch black. The road seemed to be mostly mud and ruts, and he was really young to be driving at all. His brown hair, longer than most American boys had been wearing theirs last time she paid attention, was very curly. His eyes had been blue, she remembered from that look in the hallway, and he was, she decided judiciously, cute. The accent was definitely nice, if she could get him to talk more.

"Why didn't Bes come? Are they ok?"

"Your guardian is speaking with the King. He was concerned about you, but there was much to be done, and little time."

Maybe it was because she had just been thinking about what happened that summer with the cabin, and Mars threatening her grandfather, but this gave Linn an uneasy feeling, like she was being rushed into the dark. Which she was. She gave up talking to him and stared out the window, wondering where they were going.

The place names G had given her hadn't helped a whole lot. They were supposed to be traveling to the Isle of Man, but the google view of that tiny island hadn't included a forest as large as the one they had explored that afternoon. Which meant either Ireland or Scotland, and burn meant creek, didn't it?

Merrick steered the car off the dirt road onto a proper paved road, and Linn caught the flicker of lights from a few buildings as they passed them. Now that it was smoother, and he turned up the heat, the day caught up with her, and she fell asleep watching the night slip by outside her window.

She was awakened by the jolting of the wheels hitting yet another rutted road. Linn sat up, rubbing her eyes. Merrick glanced at her. "We'll be there in a few moments."

"Thanks. Where is there?" Linn still couldn't see anything but the rutted path – this wasn't even a road! – in front of them in the headlights.

"I canna tell ye that." Merrick's accent was stronger suddenly. She looked at him in suspicion. What was he worried about?

"I don't see any lights..." Linn started to say, and then let her words trail off, because now she did see lights. They looked a lot like torches and campfires. Merrick pulled up near a low rock wall, and cut the engine.

5

UILLEAN PIPES

*T*here was music when Linn climbed stiffly out of the car. High and reedy, it didn't sound quite like bagpipes, but it swirled around her and lifted the hair on the back of her neck and made her feel... she didn't know what she was feeling, other than totally jittery and nervous. Even Blackie felt it, as he nudged his head under her hand and walked close by her while they followed Merrick toward the ring of fire.

It was, she saw as they got closer, a ring of torches stuck into ruined walls of what had been a castle keep. There was one big fire in the middle, throwing up sparks in a very messy, showy way. Linn wrinkled her nose at this display. Proper campfires didn't behave like that. It was a good way to start a forest fire, or to give away your position.

There were a lot of people around the fire, and she walked slowly toward them, assessing the situation, while her fingers tightened on Blackie's soft fur. They seemed to be having a party. There was no sign of the musician, but the wild pipes played clearly, the music both sad and joyful at once. Linn didn't think she had ever heard anything like it before. As she got closer, she could see that while there were a few women dancing, most of the people, perhaps three dozen of them crowded into the grassy hollow that would have been a Great Hall, were talking and milling around one man. He was seated on a rough-hewn bench, and talking to Bes. Bes had his back to her, his hands squarely on his hips and elbows akimbo.

Linn suppressed a smile, although no-one was looking at her even while they pushed through the crowd around Manannan Mac'Lir. Bes was not happy. He wasn't yelling, which only meant he hadn't been pushed that far yet. Mac'Lir, on the other hand, looked half asleep, his eyes hooded under bushy white eyebrows. What was it with the old gods, that they felt like they had to look so old? Was it that they felt old, worn out?

With that on her mind, she arrived next to Bes to meet the ancient god-king. Merrick swept his liege a low and surprisingly elegant bow. "I have brought her," he announced simply.

Linn didn't know what to say. Bes saved her with the introductions, "Linnea Vulkane, granddaughter of Hephaestus. Blackie, son of Sekhmet."

Blackie sat up straight and wrapped his tail around his feet, slitting his great golden eyes at the king, who nodded gravely, then lifted his gaze to Linn. His eyes, stormy as the sea he'd ruled, held hers, and she felt oddly detached from herself.

"Hello," Linn said. She was fairly sure that wasn't correct and proper, but he wasn't *her* king.

Mac'Lir smiled, and stroked his silver beard. "Hello, daughter of fire. I hear you have had an adventure."

Linn shook her head, embarrassed. "I was only separated from my traveling party."

He raised his bushy eyebrows, looking much more awake. "Not an adventure, is that?"

"I could have gone home, were I truly lost. But I was given a mission to complete."

He looked at Bes, who was doing his stone statue impersonation. Black granite, of course, Linn thought with fond amusement, doing her best to keep her thoughts from affecting her expression. Everyone was waiting for the king to speak again.

"Something makes me think you would have kept on, even had we not come to your rescue."

Linn felt a surge of indignation. She hadn't been rescued. She hadn't needed to be rescued. She pushed it down, not wanting to argue.

"I would have kept trying, yes."

"Are you willing to have a fair and true adventure, Daughter of Fire?" He tilted his head to one side, looking steadily at her. Linn felt a little awkward as everyone was quiet, waiting for her answer, and it seemed that they were all expecting something.

"I was sent by my grandfather to find out what you needed, and to provide assistance if we could." Linn knew that wasn't really an answer, but why hadn't he talked with Bes about this? Bes was the adult. She was only along as Heff's granddaughter.

"True. But amuse an old, tired man. Are you willing?" His accent was odd, she realized, listening to him. But he spoke English very well. Hadn't Grandpa said he'd been asleep for centuries?

Linn thought of the last two years, and the conversations coming to a halt with her arrival. She did want more.

"Yes."

"Ah..." He sat back and smiled. "Youth is refreshing."

Bes shifted his weight, and Linn realized guiltily that she ought to be letting him do the talking. She looked at him, and even though he hadn't changed his expression, she thought she detected approval.

"I need help, yes." Mac'Lir spoke again, and Linn paid attention to him. "My court is fallen..." He gestured loosely, at the ruins, fire, and the people who were mostly not paying too much attention to them. "Once, my rule here was supreme. The great heroes all came to eat, drink, and make merry with me. In time, I saw humanity was in ascendance."

He looked away, out into the darkness. Linn wondered when it had stopped raining, or if he was somehow keeping it from raining. He looked wistful, for those days of legend and lore. Linn remembered Hypatia talking about the dirt, disease, and despair of the past. She had no inclination to romanticize that time.

The haunting pipes filled the silence. Mac'Lir spoke again, softly. "I went with my family down to the sea, to find peace. We slept long and long in the cold, icy lands far from home. Now, I have been awoken, for what reason I know not. One calls me, from a distant shore. I am exiled from my own place..."

That explained why they weren't on the Isle of Man, then, Linn thought. She wondered when he would get to the point. One thing she had learned, these last two years, was to be patient. She waited.

"I cannot go, myself. I am needed here, I find. So, the Fire that has come to the Sea, will you go for me?"

She blinked at him. Was this what he had wanted from her grandfather? But she had said yes to the adventure. "I will go. Where, and who calls?"

"One of my blood, of my strength. They went to the new lands, after my sleep, and now all I can give you is a token, which tugs my heartstrings..."

Mac'Lir lifted a hand and held it out to her, a tiny white feather in his palm. Linn took it gently, and he cupped her hand in both of his, closing his eyes. She could see his lips moving, speaking, but couldn't hear anything. The feather grew very hot, and heavy, and Linn heard her own squeak of pain with dismay, then gritted her teeth.

Bes shifted his weight and Linn flashed a warning look at him. She'd said she would do this. He frowned, but didn't move again. The pain ebbed, and Mac'Lir let her hand go. The feather was gone. Only a blackened, ashy outline of it remained in her palm. Mac'Lir opened his eyes, smiling. Linn could see he was tired, now. Whatever he had done had been difficult.

"You will leave tomorrow, perhaps. For tonight, child, dance, refresh, and be joyful!"

Linn knew this was a dismissal, but wasn't sure quite what to do. This whole episode had been odder than even her normal. She backed away slightly, then. Bes turned away from the king, who was sitting still with his eyes closed now.

"Come on, you heard him..." Bes started, amusement in his eyes.

"I don't know how to dance..." Linn murmured to him, feeling utterly silly and blushing uncontrollably for some reason.

"We will teach you, then, Daughter of Fire!" The women who had been dancing all swooped in on her at once. Linn found herself again swept into an inexorable force as her coat came off, a long shawl was knotted around her hips to become a skirt over her practical jeans, and the pipes were joined with other instruments. She almost couldn't help it, then, the music carried her into the dance with the four women.

It was fun, she had to admit, as they took her hands, and chanted the steps for her at first. It didn't take long to learn how to follow them. Naeve, the woman with green hair, clapped her hands when she saw how quickly Linn was catching on. The music pulsed through her blood, her heart raced, and Linn whirled through the intricate patterns as her body took over from her mind.

"Faster, faster!" Naeve encouraged. They had been telling her their names, and she suspected they were naiads, except the very fair blonde with the pupil-less black eyes. That one, Ban, made Linn a little nervous when she came to her in the rounds of the dance. Now, she laughed as Linn stumbled a bit while taking her hands in turn.

"No need to fret, my pretty. I shall not sing tonight."

Linn didn't know what she meant, but this had gone from being a command, to a lot of fun, and she really did want to learn. Besides, something told her that her failure would look bad for Grandpa Heff. This was oddly important.

The pipes skirled, the drum beat faster, and Linn felt her hair slipping loose of its braid as she flew from hand to hand around the circle. The naiads were singing, softly now, a liquid chant that kept time with the fast drum, but growing louder as Linn joined in with them. She had no idea what the Gaelic words meant, but it sounded beautiful, and it felt right to sing with them. Ban, true to her promise, did not sing.

There were stars, Linn saw when she tipped her head back. Twinkling brightly overhead, and she felt like she could reach and touch them, they looked so near. Her feet kept time to the rhythm of the music, like they weren't hers, and she was part of a pattern of dancers. More had joined in, even Bes, who caught both her hands in his for a movement, his fingers warm on hers and his smile broad. He could really dance, Linn thought, and then they were separated again.

Merrick, his hair as tousled as hers must be, laughed as they danced, but she didn't mind. He wasn't laughing at her, but in joy. Everyone was happy. Mac'Lir had returned, so they celebrated.

Linn was never sure, later, how long they had danced. She knew that at some point the music had slowed, the various instruments dropping out until it was only the lonely pipes again, and then even that had stopped. The wind whispered among the stones, and she stood on the grass wondering if she had lost her mind. People were all around, some curled up near walls sleeping, others swaying with blank eyes to music only they could hear now.

Linn lifted a hand to her face, feeling her head throb. What on earth had possessed her to dance like that? And sing? She couldn't sing or carry a tune in a bucket.

Bes appeared. "Hey, now..."

He put an arm around her waist and she leaned on him. "Bes, what the hel- heck?"

"Tell you later, kiddo. You did grand." He led her toward the wall, making a gesture with his free hand. There was a doorway, with a half-open door. Blackened oak timbers, very heavy, Linn noted absently as they passed through it and into the dim room beyond.

"Was that there before?" She wasn't thinking clearly, but she was sure it hadn't been. "Where are we?"

"In the morning... well, ok, it's morning now. When you wake up."

She knew it was morning. The sun had been rising over the ruined castle wall, just the edge of dawn showing. Her head ached abominably, and she could barely keep her eyes open. Bes kept pushing her along. When the bed came into view, she stopped asking questions and let him tumble her into it. She could feel him tugging a boot off as she fell asleep, but she was past caring about being treated like a child.

6

MANANNAN'S COURT

*L*inn woke up to a pounding headache. For a fleeting moment she thought she was still hearing the drums from the night before, but then she finished waking up and realized it was her own heartbeat. She stared at the low ceiling, embossed with smoky patterns in the once-white plaster between wooden beams that looked black with age. Black with age... the door they had come through. She sat up and looked around.

Deirdre sat next to her bed, in a battered chair, reading an equally battered book. She looked up from it at Linn's movement.

"Good morning!"

Linn clutched her head. This headache was going to kill her. "Ow, ow, my head hurts."

Deirdre made a tsking sound, and produced a glass of water. "This ought to help, and these..." She handed two pills over. Linn looked dubiously at them. "Aspirin," her friend supplied. "Bes thought you would be needing it."

"How did he know?"

The water felt good, and then her stomach growled loudly, reminding her that she had eaten a handful of GORP, two cookies—biscuits—and nothing else since breakfast yesterday. Deirdre giggled. "Come on, let's find you breakfast and I'll explain."

"So last night was the first time Manannan's Court has seen him in, oh, hundreds of years." Deirdre was walking quickly, and Linn was grateful for her longer legs to keep up with the diminutive coblyn.

"Okay, so it was a party? I didn't drink anything, why do I feel like I have a hangover?" Linn wondered where Deirdre had been. She vaguely remembered seeing the big cats, perched on walls, and had she seen a wolf in the shadows, too?

"At a *feis* like this, there is a lot of magic in the air, and you weren't prepared for it. Bes said to tell you that you were drunk on Power."

"Why isn't Bes telling me this himself? Is he still asleep?" Linn's stomach rumbled harder as they found their way into a kitchen. A little woman with a face like a dried apple turned away from the big fire. Linn didn't think she had ever seen a bigger fireplace. The woman smiled and came to meet them.

"Welcome, Linnea Fire Daughter."

Linn decided she wasn't going to argue her name with the person who might feed her if she asked nicely. "Good morning."

"I am Bronwyn, welcome to my kitchen. Sit and eat, child."

Linn, gently herded in the direction of a table and chair, sat thankfully and watched as Bronwyn brought a tray. A bowl of oats, different than what oatmeal ought to look like, but smelling the same. A handful of dried apples and nuts, a little bowl with sugar, and a pitcher of cream. Along with the ubiquitous tea. Linn resigned herself to learning to enjoy the hot amber liquid.

Deirdre sat too, but didn't get a bowl, so Linn guessed she had already eaten. Linn stirred sugar, cream, and the fruit-nut mixture into her oats. It tasted delicious. Deirdre started talking again. "So, Bes had to leave..."

"What?" Linn was just happy she had swallowed right before Dee told her that. Otherwise, she might have sprayed food everywhere. "Where did he go, and why did he leave us?"

"He didn't say."

And Dee hadn't asked hard, Linn guessed. She loved the little coblyn, but the girl had been trained out of curiosity early. It couldn't be that she was born without it... Little Feagle, her baby cousin, couldn't be kept out of trouble, and Daffyd said he was just like Dee had been as a baby.

"Great." Food was most important at this second, so Linn kept eating.

"We're staying with Mac'Lir's Court until he returns." Deirdre went on, unaware of her friend's traitorous thoughts. She was pleased with her decorous behavior. "Spot and Blackie went off someplace with Merrick this morning, hunting, I think."

Linn, who liked to hunt, too, snorted with disgust at the boys cutting her out of that activity. "That means Bes will be back soon, because Mac'Lir told me I'd be leaving on my adventure today."

Deirdre got a little wide-eyed. "Leaving? Adventure?"

Linn nodded. "Evidently, he's having me stand in for Grandpa. He can't leave here, so he's sending us."

"Us?"

Linn nodded. "Aren't we a team? So that means Bes will be back soon."

"Okay." Deirdre looked dubious.

Linn finished eating. "That was really good." She looked at the empty bowl with a faint sense of surprise.

"Well, like I was trying to say before, you took part in what was practically a magical orgy last night. You burned a lot of Power."

"Er, what?" Linn was fairly sure she'd been fully dressed the whole night. She blushed again, remembering how she'd danced... and with Bes and Merrick, not just the naiads.

"Okay, maybe orgy isn't the right word."

"I hope not!" Linn made a face at her friend.

"But anyway, that's why you're hungry and all out of sorts." Deirdre wrinkled her nose. The coblyn's face was very expressive.

"I'm grumpy because I got lost, and wet, and I need a shower. Which seems unlikely in this place. I don't see running water..."

"There isn't any. I'm not sure where we are, and something makes me think we aren't on Earth."

"That would explain a lot, actually. So, no shower." Linn tried not to scratch her scalp. Just thinking about how dirty she was made her itch all over.

"We can have a bath drawn for you, child." Bronwyn was gathering her dishes, which made Linn uncomfortable. The Sanctuary ate cafeteria-style, with everyone taking their dishes to the kitchen, and the teens took turns doing assigned chores along with many adults. She was being waited on, which was an odd sensation when not at a restaurant.

"I'd appreciate that, thank you." Linn told her. "Is it something I can help with?"

Bronwyn looked amused. "No, you can just relax and it will be ready soon."

She left the dishes in the dry sink, and left the kitchen. Linn hadn't seen anyone else, and was stricken with the sudden thought that maybe Bronwyn would be doing the bath by herself. She said that out loud, and Dee shook her head.

"No, there are others serving. I think the court is slowly gathering. Mary said they were scattered to the winds, and the word of the King's return is bringing them. Merrick's family was first, of course."

"Why of course?"

Other than his grumpiness toward her in the car, Linn didn't see anything special about the boy. Well, that, and he was the youngest person of Mac'Lir's court she had seen. If there were children, they hadn't been at the... what did Deirdre call it? The *feis* last night.

"His family was the closest to the king's family, their sworn retainers. They have been awaiting his return since the last day of his rule."

"Oh, ok." Deirdre led the way back to the room they had come from. Linn thought she would just get lost; the twists and turns and narrow halls were confusing.

"Where are we?"

"Mac'Lir's castle, on the High Plane." Dee said over her shoulder. "Part of the *feis* last night was to gather the Power to open the door to Earth. This has been partially abandoned since he abdicated rule."

"And how do you know all this?" Linn finished asking as they arrived back at the room.

Deirdre looked at her in surprise. "I used to live here."

Linn felt her mouth drop open. She thought the little coblyn girl had been born in Sanctuary. Dee grinned suddenly, her eyes twinkling. She gave Linn a little push. "Wash your stinky self, and I'll tell you all about it."

Linn emerged quite a bit later, pink from the hot water and her hair hanging wet and loose. She had brushed it, but wanted to let it dry before she braided it again. If she braided it wet the waves when she unbraided were ridiculous. Between her mother's long, straight black hair inherited from Pele, and her father's curls, Linn's hair had a mind of its own at times. She had on her clean outfit from her backpack, and no idea what she was going to do about making the clothes she had been wearing clean again. For now, being clean was deliciously good.

Dee was, as usual, reading.

"What did you find?" Linn loved to read, too, but not quite as much as the little green girl.

"Tales of Gael and Loch. It's a collection of myths and legends from Scotland and Ireland."

She showed Linn the illustration of a banshee. "Recognize her?"

Linn peered at the old woodcut. "I don't think so, should I? She kills with her cry?" that was the caption given in the book.

"You were dancing with her last night." Dee giggled. "Good thing she wasn't singing."

"Oh." Linn remembered Ban, and her huge, empty black eyes, and shuddered. "She gave me the creeps."

"The banshee aren't evil, just... sad. Mostly."

"Mostly?" Linn echoed in disbelief. Then she stopped and stared. They had been walking down a hall while they chatted, and she had been letting Dee steer where they were going. Now, they stood in a huge hall. Overhead, flags hung out at an angle from the walls, so they were high overhead, but all the colors she could imagine in exotic fabrics. The tall, narrow windows with a point at the top she recognized as being gothic, and the stone floor was set into intricate patterns of different stones. The room shimmered.

"Wow..." She kept looking up, turning in place to try and take it all in.

"Come on, I want to show you the gardens." Dee headed toward a small side door.

The sunshine outside was brilliant, and it took Linn a couple of minutes to adjust to it after the relative dim of the castle. The flowers smelled wonderful, but it was the trio of approaching figures which caught her attention as soon as she could see them well enough to recognize them.

"Boys." She growled in disgust.

Blackie and Merrick flanked Spot, who looked rather misshapen. She blinked.

"What did they *catch?*"

Deirdre shaded her eyes. "Oh, goody, a stag!"

The three boys, two in cat-shape, had certainly caught something. Now that they were close, Linn decided some of that was trouble. Merrick sported a purpling shiner, and one of Blackie's eyes was swollen almost shut. Spot, on the other hand, the small deer slung over his back, neck in his mouth, was practically prancing with joy, in contrast to the two surly ones. His whiskers were spread wide, and he was grinning catlike around his mouthful.

Deirdre pointed. "Bronwyn will want that. Thank you!"

Linn addressed Blackie. "What happened to you?"

He looked away, then sat gingerly and started washing his face carefully with a paw. Merrick just glared at her.

"What?!" Linn didn't know what his problem was, either.

Linn decided to follow Spot. Maybe she could help with butchering. She somehow didn't think she was going to get an answer from them. Linn was aware the boys were following her, but she wasn't going to give them the satisfaction. Mac'Lir, however, appeared from a side path and took in the situation at a glance. With a grin and pleased tone, he exclaimed. "Boys! Good hunt!"

He was dressed in archaic clothing, a flowing white shirt and loose brown pants that had been rolled up to his knees. He was barefoot and had his hands full of green leaves. Linn eyed him with surprise. He looked nothing like the grand and mystic king of the night before. He didn't even look like the lord of the castle, but the gardener.

"Good morning." He smiled at her and held out the leaves. "Would you take these to Bronwyn?"

Linn stammered back, "Morning, and yes." She was handed an armful of wet... spinach?

"There are few enough of us, we all must do our share." Mac'Lir answered her unspoken question. "And it gives me a little quiet time to collect my thoughts."

Linn nodded, thinking about that. He'd been gone a long time, and many changes had happened. She wondered what he thought of the car.

"Go on, now." He turned back into the garden, and she kept going toward the kitchen door. It opened to Merrick's knocking, and Bronwyn appeared on the step as she opened the door. She flung up her apron with a little scream.

"Boys! You are not bringing all that mud and blood into my clean kitchen!"

Linn bit back a giggle. "I can help with butchering if there is an outside place..."

Bronwyn was surprised, she saw, at the offer. "No, no... I have kitchen helpers. But thank you."

Linn handed off her greenery. "This is from the king... he was picking it, I mean."

Bronwyn shook her head, and for some reason Linn thought that she was thinking "boys" again, in much the same way she had just spoken to the cats and Merrick. But she didn't say anything out loud, just took the greens into her apron, folded up at the bottom to make a pocket.

"Be off with you all now... Leave the deer." She pointed, and Spot laid it on the grassy patch with a last sniff of pleasure. Bronwyn shut the door on them, and the young people looked at one another.

Deirdre spoke first. "Want to see the library?"

The boys all looked at her. It was obvious to Linn that none of them had any interest in that pursuit. She knew the cat-boys avoided it on general principle, but could read for school when they had too. She had no idea about Merrick.

"Let's go see if Bes is back." Linn suggested. She was a bit antsy about their adult having gone off without them, leaving them in a strange place. It wasn't that she felt they were in any danger, but it was weird.

Bes wasn't back, and Linn wound up in the library with Deirdre anyway. The boys had vanished. Whatever they had been tussling over while out hunting, they had still bonded in some mysterious male fashion over it, leaving Linn outside their brotherhood. She was bored.

So, the summons from the king, in the form of the first child she had seen at Mac'Lir's court, came as a welcome event. He was tiny, with a nut-brown face and hair, like he spent far more time playing outside in the dirt and sunshine than he was now, dressed up in a formal page outfit and bowing stiffly.

"You are requested in the Great Hall, to attend the king's desires," he announced.

"I don't have any dress-up clothes," she told him, torn between amusement at his formal garb, and concern that she was supposed to come up with a dress or something. He didn't seem like the kind of king who stood on protocol... she remembered the garden encounter that morning.

"As you are." The little boy told her pompously.

"Well, then..." she stood up. "Let's go."

Deirdre followed as well. They came to the Great Hall of flags, where Manannan Mac'Lir was seated on a carved wooden throne, with a small group of people around him. Some were standing and talking, others were at two tables, sitting and writing on paper. Linn had a fleeting thought to wonder what the king would think of a computer. She hadn't brought her laptop along.

She stopped when the page stopped. He executed a neat little bow, and she looked up at Mac'Lir. "Am I supposed to curtsey or something?"

He laughed. "No, I know you aren't my subject, and besides, you are charmingly different my dear."

"I'm an American." Linn shrugged. "I know what a king is, but I've never had one."

He nodded. "Much has changed since I laid down to sleep. I am learning, but it will take time. Which I don't have to spare."

"I'm not sure how I can help, until Bes gets back." Linn shrugged.

Mac'Lir looked surprised. "Have you looked at your hand?"

"Wha-" She looked at her palm, where he had put the feather last night. There was a black mark there, in the shape of a feather. "You tattooed me!"

"Not exactly. It will fade in time. I used the feather to give you all you needed to complete your quest. Then, you may return to me, having proven yourself, and I will grant your wish." He leaned back in his throne, doing that sleepy-eyed contemplation of her again. Linn opened her mouth to give him a piece of her mind, and then shut it again.

This was, after all, what she had wanted. She'd volunteered for it.

"Am I going alone, then?" Linn really didn't want that.

Mac'Lir shook his head, smiling. "You may take whomever you like. But you must go within the hour. I will also send Merrick with you, of my household. He is close to my heart, and will make a good champion for you."

Linn felt her mouth drop open again, and made herself close it quickly. Of all the people she *didn't* want, Merrick topped the list. Not that he'd done anything wrong, but... he annoyed her. She turned and looked at Deirdre.

"Do you want to come?" Linn asked her.

Dee shook her head, looking sad. "I'm not ready for that kind of adventure, I'm sorry."

"Oh, Dee..." Linn hugged her impulsively. "It's ok. You don't have to if you don't want to. I'm the one that volunteered. I'll leave Spot with you, so you aren't on your own until Bes gets back."

Dee nodded, her eyes a little watery. "Thanks. I'm not alone, but..."

Linn nodded. She knew she wouldn't want to be alone in a place full of people she didn't know. She turned back to Mac'Lir.

"I have to get my pack, and I am ready."

"Brave girl. You are to go where the feather takes you, and return with the one who seeks my ruling. They cannot travel here on their own, they have not the strength."

Linn could feel the palm of her hand grow warm as he channeled a little Power into it. The tiny nanobots, a legacy of a civilization so far in advance of humans as to appear magical, might be invisible, but they had a lot of strength even after all these centuries. Linn's hypothesis was they were self-replicating, but on a very limited level, or the gods would have taken over Earth a long time ago instead of retreating as humans developed tech of their own.

But for now, she clenched her hand around the mark he'd made, and nodded goodbye before retreating to the room where she had left her things. Someone had taken her dirty clothes, and they were folded neatly and clean on the bed. A cloth-wrapped bundle proved to be food when she investigated, and her water bottle had been refilled. Linn wasn't sure whether she was upset someone had touched her things, or happy for the help. This whole trip had her off balance – it had from the beginning when she'd been separated from Bes on the High Path.

Hopefully that wouldn't happen this time. She was going to take Blackie, and had to take Merrick, and who knew if he could walk the High Path. He'd come to get her in a car, after all. Linn sighed and put her backpack on. Time to get this done. Maybe it would be easy.

7

ANSWERING THE CALL

*M*errick met her and Blackie by the door to the garden.
"Have you ever taken the High Path?" Linn asked him. He was dressed in a very modern jacket layered over a t-shirt and jeans. Hiking boots completed the ensemble. At least he looked like he could pass as normal. Blackie, on the other hand... Linn sighed. She really didn't know what to do about the big cat. He looked like an escapee from the zoo.

Merrick answered her. "Yes, but only with someone else. I don't have the power to do it myself." He looked like he'd bitten into a lemon. Linn guessed it was hard on his pride to admit that.

"I can, now, and I couldn't before, so maybe you can learn." She offered a good thought for him.

He shrugged and turned away. "Where are we going?"

"I have no idea." Linn held out her hand. "But it's time."

Blackie nudged his head under her hand, and Merrick slowly held out his for her to take. She closed her eyes, gathered a sense from the feathermark on her hand of time and place, and then took a big step. When she opened her eyes again, they were on the Path. "Keep moving," she warned the others, having learned her lesson well. "I don't know how long this will take."

Merrick just grunted acknowledgment, looking around. He hadn't let go of her hand, either. Linn could feel the feather tattoo pulsing in time with her heart.

"Why are you mad?" Linn decided she would make conversation to pass the time.

Merrick looked startled. She went on. "Is it because Mac'Lir asked you to take care of me? Because I can take care of myself."

"No... I don't mind that," he said.

"You were fighting with Blackie." Linn could feel Blackie twitch his shoulders, like he was trying to knock off a fly. Merrick looked amused.

"We were just messing around. It's a guy thing."

"I don't understand guys." Linn stuck her tongue out at him.

Merrick took a deep breath, and then burst into laughter. "I don't understand girls, either. You're ok, though."

"Gee, thanks. Ouch." Her hand was suddenly burning. She let go of Merrick's hand and shook it in the air. "Ow!"

He looked alarmed. "I felt that."

"It hurts!" Linn thought quickly. "Let's get off the High Path."

It was hard to collect her thoughts and land them, with her hand throbbing, but they stepped out into a... strip mall parking lot? She looked around. It was nighttime, and the parking lot was lit with only one streetlight, which was flickering like it was about to go out. The stores were dark, and she didn't think most of them would be open even in the daytime.

"Where *are* we?" Merrick asked.

"I don't know. But my hand feels better." She shivered. The night air was cool, and she was worried about someone seeing Blackie.

"Can you use it to figure out if we are close?" Merrick had turned so he could see behind them, and Blackie was looking out into the darkness as well. Linn decided she could risk closing her eyes and using the sight to try figuring this out.

When she focused, she could feel a mental tugging off to her left. She looked.

"Well, I think we need to go around this." Since she was fairly sure that what they were looking for wasn't inside that store, with the boarded-up windows. And what kind of name was "Shur-Sav?"

"Before someone sees us." Merrick looked as uneasy as she felt.

The alley behind the stores was completely dark, and pitted with potholes that Linn was having trouble avoiding. Merrick and Blackie started steering her around them after she stepped in the first one.

"You ok?" Merrick asked in a low tone.

"Fine..." Linn whispered back. Her ankle hurt, but not badly. The dark was spooking her.

Her eyes adjusted to the dark slowly, and they walked along the back wall. Linn wasn't sure what they were looking for, but when she saw the pinpoints of light around the door, she was sure that had to be it. She walked up to it and knocked. Out of the corner of her eyes she saw Blackie fade into the shadows.

Good, she still wasn't one hundred percent sure this is where they were supposed to be. She could hear footsteps approaching the door. It jerked open, inward, and bright light spilled out over her and Merrick, standing just behind and slightly to one side.

"Who t'hell are you?" The man with the gun demanded.

Linn eyed it. That shotgun barrel looked monstrously big from this side. He held it low, and with his finger on the trigger. She flared her hands out to the sides, holding them so it was obvious they were empty. She really, really hoped Merrick didn't do anything silly.

"Mac'Lir sent us." She spoke softly, meeting his eyes and hoping he had a clue what she was talking about.

He blinked rapidly. Then he leaned forward, peering around them, and making Linn very nervous as the barrel of the gun approached her sternum. Behind her, she could hear a low growl from Merrick.

"Get in here." The man ordered, with a jerk of the gun barrel. He stepped back slightly to allow them past, but kept the weapon pointed at the teenagers. Linn was having second and even third thoughts at this point, but she stepped past him into the empty storeroom. Merrick followed, and she could see now that he had followed her lead, keeping his hands well away from his body and conspicuously empty.

"Who are you?" The man demanded again. Now another man walked through the hanging plastic strips from the main part of the store, also carrying a gun. Linn's heart sank.

"I think we may be in the wrong place." She told them, trying to keep her voice level and calm. "We came from Manannan Mac'Lir in response to a call for help."

Linn didn't dare close her eyes and look to see if either of them had an aura of power. She kept eye contact with the first man, waiting to see what he would do. He looked at the second man.

"D'ye think they're cops?"

The second man snorted and shook his head in disgust. "Sometimes I think Mama dropped you on your head. They're kids. Tie them up, and then we can figger out what t'do with them."

Linn held very still as the man tied Merrick hand and foot, then her. She wasn't about to try and be heroic with that gun trained on them both. To her relief, Merrick didn't, either. If their captors left them alone, she could get them out of the mess she'd gotten them into. Once they were both bound and lying on the cold concrete floor, the second man dropped the muzzle of his gun, and walked over to the first one. Faster than she could really see, he drove the butt of the shotgun into the younger man's belly.

"You idiot!" He screamed as the first one folded up onto the floor, keening with pain.

Linn laid still and pretended to be not-there, hard. Older man, clean shaven, but with long greasy gray hair tied back into a queue, kept yelling.

"What are you gonna do with them, huh? It's one thing to have a lab right here in town, it's a whole 'nother thing to dispose of two kids!"

Linn shivered. The man kept ranting. "You and your stupid chants. Every stinking time something goes wrong, you call on Mac'Lir, like he's a real god, or something. Now look what you've done!"

Linn closed her eyes. Partly, this was to try and suppress the nervous giggle she could feel welling up inside her. Either the guy's chanting had worked, or it hadn't... and her arrival kind of proved it did. The other reason she closed her eyes was to focus her inner sight and see what power they might have.

The man on the floor had a flicker of Mac'Lir's sea green power, not a lot. The other one had nothing. She thought she could guess why they were here... and it made her very curious about how this whole summoning thing worked. For instance, would it call her grandfather if she did it to him? It wasn't like all the gods were linked by their nanotech, or they couldn't have fought for centuries without at the least, telegraphing their every move to their opponents.

Linn had spent the last two years studying the power of the gods in her spare time around school, and playing on the beach. She knew it was leftover technology so advanced as to look like magic. What she didn't know, yet, was how to properly use it and possibly replicate it. That, she had decided almost as soon as she had guessed what it was, she would make her life's work as she grew up.

Right now, she was just hoping she'd have the time to continue those studies. The man was done shouting, and she could hear one set of steps leaving the room. The man who was related to Mac'Lir was sitting up slowly. Linn peeked, not fully opening her eyes.

He wasn't looking at them as he held his stomach and got to his feet. He left the room, gun lying on the floor behind him, and Linn saw Merrick start to wriggle toward it.

"Shh! Wait!" She cautioned him.

"What?" he hissed back through clenched teeth.

"What are you going to do with it? Let me get us untied first." Linn concentrated, imaging her rope as she felt the knots. "This might take a minute..."

"What are you doing?" He was trying to keep his voice down, but failing.

"I'll explain later!" Linn told him with exasperation. She could feel the tingle of something happening to the rope, but she didn't dare hurry it, as it got hotter when she tried that.

In the other room, there was a sudden tinkle of breaking glass, and voices swearing. Linn risked her hands burning, silently concentrating hard on the rope. She could feel it... dissolving. Just as it dropped away, the men came stumbling through the curtain with a truly horrible reek, coughing.

Neither of them was carrying a gun now, but she still didn't want to challenge them. They were bigger than she was, and Merrick was still helpless. Linn lay very still and hoped that they couldn't see her hands behind her back.

The bigger man sideswiped at the other one. "You moron! That's tonight's work you done wasted. And we still gotta git rid of these two."

"All right, all right! I'm sorry... Let's get out of here for a while. I need fresh air." The man who had met them at the door headed for it now.

"What about them?" Big man pointed.

"I don't know. Not now..." he was gagging as he swung the door opened. And then he screamed like a little girl, jumping backwards. He tripped over Merrick's legs and fell awkwardly, his arms flailing.

Linn could barely see, her eyes were streaming with tears from the fumes. There was a figure in the doorway, a human shape, so it wasn't Blackie. In the confusion, maybe it was time to escape. She shoved a hand in her pocket, fumbling for the little knife Bes had given her.

Neither of the men seemed to even see her as she belly-crawled ungracefully to Merrick and sawed at his ropes.

"Don't move! This is really sharp!" she murmured in his ear. He held obligingly still, and she only cut him a little as the rope let go.

He doubled up and she reached for his legs, then felt a terrible blow to the back. The big man had noticed her, and kicked her, hard. Linn rolled on the floor, gasping and gagging. Between the pain and the fumes, she had lost track of Merrick, and her knife.

There was a scream from the doorway, but she couldn't see what was happening. Beside her there was a low growl.

"Blackie!" she squeaked. Her voice was hoarse and raw.

A new voice entered her awareness, reverberating, and oozing with power. "Still."

Everyone stopped moving. Linn gasped for air, feeling her face covered in snot and tears, a cool draft on the wetness of it. Footsteps moved closer, and she could hear the voice, firm, female, and mature, speaking softly in a language she didn't recognize. Then it switched over to English, and Linn could follow the conversation.

"Will, Chad; what do you have to say for yourselves?" the voice commanded.

The two men spoke at once, their words tripping over one another. "Granny Clinch! Don't curse us..."

"We're just tryin' to make a living..."

"We meant them no real harm..."

"Will's a moron."

"Chad wanted to kill them!"

Granny Clinch, Linn supposed, spoke no louder than before, but the voice commanded and rang from the walls. "Silence. You have made trouble for the family for the last time."

Now, Linn could see through her tears as the old woman bent over her. "Can you stand?" She asked Linn.

Linn rolled onto her side, then tried to get up. She felt fur under her fingertips and latched onto it gratefully. She still couldn't see well, and the guidance to open air was very helpful. Outside in the dark, she was guided to the tailgate of a truck, and sat on it, wiping her tears off her cheeks and trying to resist the urge to rub her eyes. There was a train rumbling past, on the embankment behind the stores she had glimpsed while they were walking around. Between that noise, and her eyes, she felt very helpless.

The train went on forever. She had mostly gotten her eyes clear, but it was still very dark in the alley. The open doorway was a rectangle of dim light, but if there were voices, she couldn't hope to hear them. Linn wasn't even sure she would hear a gunshot. Surely a shotgun blast would be louder than the train?

Finally, a silhouette appeared in the doorway. As she walked toward the truck, Blackie joined her, the big cat unmistakable in the backlighting. Linn looked down in confusion at the big beast lying beside her on the tailgate. A silvery-gray ruff glimmered in the light. Big eyes gleamed, and a tail thumped on the bed behind her. This was a very large wolf.

"Now, who are you?" Linn asked.

"Good question for all of you." This could only be the woman the men had called Granny Clinch. Her hair, lit from behind, glowed like a white halo, or a dandelion puff. Linn couldn't see her face, her expression, but the tone of voice was not happy.

Linn swallowed hard. They had stumbled into something over their heads, and this might not be the rescue it had felt like at first.

"I'm Linnea Vulkane..." She offered, quietly.

"And I'm Mary Talon Clinch. Now, get in the truck. Boys, ride in the back." Granny Clinch didn't even hesitate, just went around and got in, saying over her shoulder. "Close the gate, girl."

Linn banged it up and shook it, in case it was like Grandpa Heff's tailgate, which fell down if it wasn't latched just right. Then she climbed into the cab while Blackie leapt into the bed of the truck to sit with the wolf. Merrick? Granny had called him boy, and Merrick wasn't in sight.

"Where are we going?" She wasn't entirely sure she should just trust any adult, and what had happened to the men in the abandoned store?

"My place. We'll talk when we get there. And I know your grandfather, child. Rest your mind."

Linn decided that the only way Granny Clinch would know who her grandfather was, was to have looked at her with Sight and interpreted Linn's power signature. Which still didn't mean that she was a good guy. It did mean that she was worth talking to. When she was ready, because she had fallen silent, looking at the road and paying no attention to Linn. In the light from the dashboard, Linn could see that she was old, which made sense with Granny being her identity to those grown men.

How old, on the other hand, she couldn't possibly guess. Heff and Pele had been on Earth for thousands of years, but they chose what age they looked. Recently, a lot younger, which made Linn happy. They looked old, she had decided, when they felt tired and old. Bes had proven that by youthening when she challenged him about his white hair.

Which meant Granny Clinch could be old in human terms, or in the gods'. Linn wondered absently what the gods had called themselves before they had come to Earth. They seemed to hold themselves separate from 'human' but they could have babies with humans. How different could they be? If it was only the nanobots, the tiny computers which could give them so much power, then getting rid of those would make them only human.

Linn wondered if the weapon she had helped developed would ever be used, and how wide the range would be. If it were detonated near Hawaii, would it hurt her grandparents and mother? Or the coblyns? And where had the coblyns come from, anyway? That had never occurred to her before today.

Linn started making a mental list of questions to ask when she got home. The silence and the darkness got to her, and the heat being turned up, and she nodded off into sleep before they had gone very far.

8

GRANNY

*L*inn jolted awake when the truck turned off the smooth paved road and onto a rough one. Blinking, she rubbed her eyes and regretted that when she was reminded of the earlier damage to them by a flash of pain and a flood of tears. She sniffed, fluttering her hands a little as she resisted rubbing more.

"You okay?" Granny Clinch asked, her voice gentler now.

"My eyes... I'm okay. Just it's making my nose run."

Granny Clinch chuckled softly. "Napkins in the glove compartment."

Linn gratefully mopped her face and blew her nose. "Where are we?" She looked around. It was near dawn, she guessed, as the light was starting to gleam through the trees that surrounded the road, making everything look gray.

"Just about there. You know we're in Kentucky, right?"

Linn shook her head. "I've never been to Kentucky before. We just went where the token from Manannan Mac'Lir sent us."

"So Mac'Lir has awakened?" Granny Clinch turned into a driveway. "Timing is... interesting, on that. I wonder why now?"

Linn didn't know. She did know she was groggy, hungry, and had no idea where they were, besides at a small house in a dark forest. She was beginning to feel like they had somehow slipped into a fairy tale.

"Come in, child, and I will get breakfast into all of you. Then we need to talk."

Linn was grateful for this respite, even if she still wasn't sure she would be able to provide all the answers. Food and time to collect her thoughts would be good. It had been an eventful and stressful night.

"What happened to those men?" She asked, climbing out of the truck and watching Blackie and Merrick frolic. This explained a lot, right here, and how could they be having fun when she felt like she had been beaten with sticks?

"'Bout now, the sheriff will be talking to them. I left them sitting and thinking about what they had done, while they waited for him to show up. It will be a long time before they come back around, with that meth lab they were working in all laid out for the sheriff to find like that."

"Oh." Linn hadn't realized that was what they were doing. She'd seen a special on TV about it. No wonder the fumes had made her so sick. They could have killed her, or exploded and killed them all. "I'm sorry."

Granny Clinch stopped in the hall and looked at her in surprise. "Why are you sorry?"

"Your grandsons..." Linn wasn't sorry they were busted over the drugs; that was good. But it had to be hard to turn in family like that.

Granny sniffed and opened the door into the main house. "Take off your shoes. Will you eat biscuits and gravy?"

"I'll eat whatever is put in front of me, Ma'am." Linn assured her.

"You call me Granny. Plates are in there, set the table while I start gravy." Linn headed for the cupboard indicated, deciding that unlike all the gods she had met, this one scared her. Also, she thought it would be a very bad idea indeed to call her a god.

It took surprisingly little time to make the food, although Linn was long finished with setting when the timer rang and the pan of golden-brown biscuits came out.

"Call in the boys, please." Granny was whisking the gravy.

Linn's stomach was telling her that it was dying. Agony, oh agony! She scooted and called out the door. "Blackie, Merrick! Breakfast!"

They appeared out of the woods, leaping over a flowerbed smoothly without ruffling a petal, the big silvery gray and black bodies moving fast and in perfect tandem. Linn felt a little envy, both for the speed of animal-shape, and their apparent decision to make friends.

"C'mon, guys." She held open the door, and they padded down the hall ahead of her. Granny met them at the inner door, wiping her hands on a dishtowel.

"Change for the table, boys. Linn, give them some privacy."

Linn, startled, went into the kitchen and Granny closed the door behind them. "Granny... Blackie doesn't..."

The door opened, and Linn turned to look. Merrick, back to brown-haired boy form, with jeans and a t-shirt. The shirt looked like it was from some band Linn didn't know. Behind him was Blackie. Linn felt her jaw drop.

Blackie had never, to her knowledge, shifted to human form. She wasn't really sure he could do it. Some of the old gods had only beast forms, or at best part-human. The minotaur, centaurs, mermaids... Even though both Sekhmet and Steve could do human and beast, their children had only shifted to human under extreme duress, and then only the two who were traumatized. Pat and Moira were lovely little girls, human form with no apparent ability to shift back to their kitten form, and physically about three years old. Linn was very fond of them. Blackie and Spot had gotten much, much bigger in these two years.

Still, she had no idea that translated to 'grown-up' in human form. Here he was, taller than Merrick, dark haired and with a shadow of beard. Blackie was wearing dark slacks and a white shirt, with a bright painted tie to add color. He looked an awful lot like Steve, Linn concluded numbly.

"Sit, sit..." Granny was bustling around putting things on the table. The biscuits, gravy, a jug of milk and a carafe of coffee. From somewhere she had produced a pitcher of juice, and sausages on the side for the boys. She raised an eyebrow at Linn, who declined with a head shake. She didn't diet, but she tried not to eat everything she saw, either.

Linn sat, still stunned by Blackie's transformation. The boys shuffled into their chairs, with sidelong glances at Linn. She was waiting for Blackie to say something. What would his voice sound like? They had communicated by gesture and eye contact for so long... she met his eyes.

He smiled, and tilted his head slightly. Linn felt a rush of relief. It was really him, and he was feeling as weird as she was.

Her moment over, the stomach spoke up again, and Linn obeyed Granny's order to 'help yourself' with all speed. No one talked while they were eating. The boys put away a lot of food, and Linn realized that Granny's big batch of biscuits was about right. She'd been thinking that was an awful lot of food, but it disappeared.

After they had all finished, Linn got up, feeling a little odd, but determined to help with the dishes. Strange kitchens put her off balance, but her mother had always told her to be helpful when she could. Granny Clinch showed her where the supplies were, and pointed to Merrick.

"You dry. And you, young man, I have a chore for."

Blackie took the broom meekly. Linn wondered when the big talk was going to happen, but this felt easy and domestic in comparison. You could almost pretend, she thought as she handed a plate to Merrick, that they were a normal family, brothers and sister.

It helped, a little, to distract her from wondering what Granny really was, and what she would want. It also helped to distract her from thinking about what Mac'Lir would say when they got back. She didn't think this was the adventure she was supposed to have. There was no success here, she hadn't done anything.

When Granny finally beckoned them to follow her out onto the front deck of the house, overlooking a deep ravine filled with trees, brush, and flowers, Linn was glad enough to follow. All three young people went to the railing and looked over it. There were birds and butterflies everywhere, under the blue sky and sunlight. It was still morning, from the position of the sun.

"Come and sit, it's time to talk." Granny Clinch was already sitting at the round, glass-topped table. Linn took a chair next to her, and the boys sat across from them. "Well, now... You're the spokeswoman, aren't you, girl?"

Linn nodded and opened her mouth. "I'm not really sure where to start."

Granny nodded and smiled, just a little. "It will come to you."

Linn looked at Merrick, and Blackie. "Well, about two years ago I didn't know I was the granddaughter of two gods, and I thought he was a perfectly ordinary kitten when I met him..."

It took a while to tell the whole story. Granny would occasionally ask her questions and make her go into more detail. The boys sat and listened quietly, looking interested. Linn realized that Blackie might never have heard the whole story before. He'd been with her for part of it, sure, but when had he been 'grown' enough to be aware? He'd looked new-born when she first met him.

Merrick, of course, would have had no idea about all of this, nor should Granny, although as Linn got to the part of bringing all the god's children from around the world to Sanctuary for protection, she nodded. Linn wondered if she had heard something about that operation.

Linn hesitated as she got to the weapon. It wasn't her secret to reveal, and not something any enemy should know about. She decided it wasn't necessary, and skipped to the part where Blackie took her on the High Path to rescue Bes. Merrick and Granny looked at him, and Linn watched with fascination as he blushed. He got up and went to lean over the railing, hiding his face.

Linn ran the whole last two years together in a tangle of sentences, feeling her throat hurting from talking for so long, and fell silent. Granny got up and went into the house. Linn stood up and went to lean on the railing, bumping shoulders with Blackie affectionately.

"Can you talk?" she asked, curious.

"Yeah," he answered gruffly, looking intently down into the brush below them.

"Could you before?"

He looked at her sideways, then back down. "I don't think so."

"Okay." Linn lapsed back into silence.

Granny came back out, and Linn turned around. The old woman was carrying a stack of plastic cups and a pitcher full of what was probably iced tea. It was. Linn appreciated it on her throat.

"What happened to the children who came to Sanctuary?" Granny asked.

"They stayed a few months, some longer than others, until the elders decided the battle on the High Plane had satisfied the Old gods, and they were cleared to go home again," Linn answered.

"And when hostilities erupt again?" Granny poured herself more tea.

Linn shrugged. "I'm a kid, they don't talk to me about it, much."

"Yet you were sent to Mac'Lir when he called."

"Yeah, because we didn't know what he wanted, and..." she hesitated, then decided to reveal the other part. "Something came up, urgent, and the adults had to go look into that. Bes was with me at first. I don't know where he went."

Linn was still worried over that. It was unlike him to take off, and although she felt it meant he trusted her to be responsible, it was a little alarming to feel like a baby bird kicked out of the nest. She wasn't sure she was ready to fly.

"Mac'Lir sent you on a quest. Do you know what that means?" Granny asked, leaning back in her chair.

Linn shook her head. "I don't know Mac'Lir at all. He's..." She wasn't sure how to politely explain.

Granny Clinch looked at Merrick. "You know."

He nodded. Granny lifted her eyebrows at him, and he ducked his head, looking embarrassed. Granny Clinch spoke very softly, and Linn almost couldn't hear her.

"Your family has served him for long and long. He has not forgotten that, nor will he. Thy great-grand's sacrifices bled blood intermingled with all Manannan held dear. He cannot put that aside, lad."

Merrick took a deep breath and looked like the wolf he shifted to, alert and powerful. "He's testing us. He doesn't mind that Hephaestus sent his granddaughter; it is blood of his blood. But Manannan Mac'Lir has always been cautious with his trust, and he cannot simply say what he needs, until he knows the messenger is trustworthy."

"Oh." Linn thought of the meth lab, and the men. Of being bound on the floor along with Mac'Lir's emissary. She'd failed already.

Her disappointment must have showed on her face. Merrick went on, his voice gloomy. "I failed him. I let us walk right into danger without protecting you, and then I couldn't rescue you once we were there."

Granny shook her head and cackled with laughter. "Young'uns, you take all this so seriously. Girl, why did you knock on that door?"

Linn lifted her hand of the arm of the chair and looked at the perfect feather tattoo in her palm. "Well, Mac'Lir gave me this as a guide."

She leaned over and Granny Clinch took her hand, fumbling for her reading glasses that hung from a cord around her neck. Her hands felt leather-tough on Linn's. Once she could see clearly, Granny looked at the feather for a long time, then closed her eyes. Linn guessed she was using the Sight to see the magical talisman.

"You did as you were directed. Mac'Lir, hasty as ever..." The old lady sniffed loudly in disdain. "Had he scryed the calling first, he would have seen it was a foolish child calling as he had done for years, and his father before him. A call meant to be used only in extremity, perverted to a good-luck chant."

"Oh." Linn really wasn't sure what to say in response to this. So, the feather had worked, and she had gone where she was supposed to. Into a danger unseen.

Merrick was the next target. Granny Clinch shook one bony finger at him. "And you, you need to learn to treat your gifts as that, not curses. Nothing wrong with who you are born to be, stop trying to be normal, child!"

Merrick squirmed. Linn looked away, the only thing she could do to give him some space. Granny Clinch went on, inexorable.

"Both of you are being silly. You didn't need rescuing. I was on my way as soon as I got the distress call, but had I been five minutes later you would have been out of there. You..." she pointed at Linn. "You were prepared, and kept your head under fire."

She turned the finger on Merrick again, who flinched a little. "And all you had to do was take wolf-form, and the bindings would have dropped away. Work on keeping your cool, lad. It's the best weapon, keeping your head."

Now Linn could feel herself blushing. Blackie interjected, shyly. "And me?"

Granny Clinch got up and hugged him. "You called me. Good lad for not charging into a situation half-cocked."

"Come on, then." The old woman walked through the open door. "Lunch. I remember that age..." her voice trailed away as she got out of hearing range.

Linn was hungry, so she followed, wanting to help in return for her meal. Just like before, Granny Clinch put all three of them to work. Linn was peeling apples, and she focused on her task, but started to talk.

"Granny, what is your connection to Mac'Lir?"

"Stories after meal," that personage replied, stirring another pot of tea with ice.

This meal was quicker: sandwiches, tea, and the fruit went into pies for later. Granny led them all back onto the deck, and when they were settled, she began, gazing out into the green forest below them.

"In the time of the Tuatha De Danaan, the gods ruled over mortals. In time, the humans grew strong, and saw that this was not the way they wanted to continue on. While all, mortals and the ever-living, gathered at the great Fair on the banks of the River Blackwater, the mortals drew their hidden weapons and drove the ever-living from the face of the earth. The Tuatha De Danaan withdrew into the *sidhe,* and ere long, from the memories of the mortals. Only the legends lived on, and they became changed from tellings and retellings.

"In the *sidhe*, which you younglings know as the High Plane, and apart from this world, the ever-living hid. There, the immortal beings drew inward, hurt, and their politics grew ever more complex. Into this, Manannan Mac'Lir, the god of all oceans, was drawn as into a whirlpool. His family suffered for it. His wife, Fand, wanted to desert him for another. I will draw a veil over all that happened then, for the sake of your young ears."

Granny chuckled, and Linn decided she really didn't want to know. She knew all about sex, but it didn't interest her in the slightest. Some things were just gross.

Granny Clinch went on, her eyes dreamy with long-ago memories, and Linn realized that she had a melodic Irish accent now, while she was telling the old tales. "After that time, Manannan returned to Earth, but lived in secret, the last of the ancients in the Isles once so beloved of them who had now become *Sidhe.* Even though he was meek and mild - saving only for releasing his anger into the sea, to rise as storms - the island where he dwelled became known by his name."

"The Isle of Man." Linn murmured. Granny nodded and took a drink.

"There were a few more adventures, and the legends always lived on. But with the coming of Christ to the Isles, and Mac Cuill's conversion, Mac'Lir retreated again from Earth. In time, tired and worn, he went to a secret place only he knew, and slept, with his wife and children beside him."

Granny closed her eyes, her face slack and grey, and Linn wondered if she herself had dropped off into a nap. She looked at Merrick, and Blackie, who had been as interested as she in the old woman's tales of Mac'Lir.

Granny sighed, and opened her eyes again. "You asked about me. I am one who was of Aoife's blood, one of the swan maidens. When the ancient ones passed from the face of the earth, not all of the ever-living chose to follow them into the *sidhe*. Still others were expelled from that refuge, or fled its oppressions and conflicts to wander Earth once again.

"I am one of those, and connected to Manannan by the swan's blood, so I may call on him, and be called in return. My family, those who were born of my blood, can as well. Which is how you came here. Do you know the tale of the swan's skin, child?"

This was directed at Linn, who shook her head. She hadn't paid a lot of attention to the Celtic tales, except the bits about coblyns, goblins, and brownies, because of her friends.

"There is a terrible tale," Granny began.

To Linn's surprise, Merrick made a little growl in the pit of his throat, and a thundercloud look came over his face. Granny laughed.

"Wolfling, be not so hasty to wrath! Let me tell the tale, and perhaps you will learn a thing or two about the king you love all unknowing."

Merrick subsided, still frowning, and Granny grew serious again.

"The tale goes that Mac'Lir, in a fit of wrath, killed his wife. She was in swan form, they say, and when she was dead, he was seized with a fit of remorse. He wept over her body for days, and then he skinned her and cured the skin. Finally, he made a magical bag from the swan, in her shape."

Merrick wriggled in his chair, and Linn could see he was trying not to explode in anger. She could see why; this was a horrible story.

Granny's voice went all soft. "It wasn't true. Mac'Lir could no more kill his beloved wife than he could himself. And he tried that, often enough, before Niamh of the Fair Hair got through his thick skull."

Now her voice was back to the soft southern accent Linn had first heard from her. "His daughter was the one who pointed out that the body had not been found, only blood, and the swan's skin cape we all used to conceal our true forms from mortals when we wished."

"And that is what he made into the bag where anything desired could be drawn forth." Merrick's voice was a little rough, like he had been crying, but Linn hadn't seen tears. She sort of understood that, though. It was a terrible thing to think about someone you respected as much as she had seen Merrick act toward the king.

Linn wrinkled her forehead in thought. "Wait a minute. I thought you said that Mac'Lir's wife had gone to sleep with the rest of the family in the secret place."

The oven timer for the pies went off, startling all of them. Linn felt herself jump, even though she knew immediately what it was.

9

GUARDIANS

*W*hen Granny had vanished into the house, Linn looked at Merrick. "You okay?"

He nodded. "Yeah. I didn't know... I was afraid she was going to say it was true."

Merrick got up and leaned on the railing. "If she said it was true, I was going to have to believe her."

"Oh." Linn tried to think about this applied to Grandpa Heff. "What did she mean about your great grand's blood, this morning?"

He looked at her. "It's how my family came to be in Mac'Lir's service. When his first wife died, his second wife resented the children he already had, even though they were her nephews and niece. So she started trying to come up with ways to get rid of them. There was a wolf-pack that roamed near the castle, and she told Mac'Lir she was living in fear of the wolves attacking. He allowed her to bring in two great hounds to stand guard in the nursery.

"He was away one day, and when he came back, he went straight to the nursery, as was his habit. To his horror, he found blood spatter on the stairs up to the tower where he'd left the children playing. He raced up the stairs, finding more and more blood, then the broken body of a wolf.

Mac'Lir drew his sword, and leapt through the open door into the nursery. What he found there turned his blood to ice.

"The two hounds were in pieces, strewn about the floor. Four wolves were in the room, dead, or dying. Blood dripped from the ceiling, falling into Mac'Lir's eyes, but his tears cleared them again. There was no sign of his children anywhere, except the carnage that might have been their blood as well. He saw the largest of the wolves lying on the floor move a little, and he lifted the great sword he carried, the one which could cut through anything, and prepared to drive it into the beast's heart.

"The blood dripped in his eye again, and as he brought the sword down, he missed entirely, and only cleaved the thick boards of the floor. Then the wolf staggered to his feet, and Mac'Lir saw that the gray beast had hidden the children beneath him, and they leapt up now, seeing they were safe, and hugged both their father, and the wolf, pleading Mac'Lir not to kill it.

"Later, the story they told him while the wolf was carried to the Great Hall and had his wounds tended delicately, was of the hounds setting on them. They hid under a bed, and peeping out while the dogs scratched and raged in vain, being too large to fit under, they saw the wolf-pack charge into the room. The wolves fought valiantly, until they too were killed. In the battle, the bed was upset, and the great wolf lay over them protecting them with his own body. When he went limp, the children were sure he was dead, and then Mac'Lir had come in."

Merrick fell silent, looking off into the distance. The day had grown hazy with the heat of the sun, and the hills had gone from green to shadowed blue. Granny Clinch spoke behind them.

"You tell the story well, lad. That wolf was your ancestor, and your family has been devoted to Mac'Lir for centuries."

Linn had guessed that part. "But why did they protect the children?"

"The wolves had a *geas* set on them. They were in the area to watch Aoife, Mac'Lir's new wife."

That was Granny Clinch. Merrick turned around and stared at her. "How do you know that? They didn't even know that until much later, and we are forbidden to talk about it."

"I knew who put it on them." She answered calmly. "Who wants more tea?"

Blackie, who had been curled catlike in his chair, long legs half-pulled up, stretched. "May I..." He stopped, as they all looked at him. He looked flustered. "I need..."

"Ah. Yes, yes, boy, go do what you need. We'll keep the juicy stories for when you get back."

Granny settled back into her chair with a sigh.

Linn came and sat on the deck by her, looking up at her. "I have a question."

Granny raised her eyebrows. "Full of them, I'd imagine. And why are you cozying up to me?"

Linn felt her cheeks heat up. "You remind me of the other grandmother. Not Pele... she's..."

Her maternal grandmother was as volatile and fiery as her persona of volcano and war goddess would imply. Linn didn't remember her father's mother well, but she did remember playing with dolls, at Nona's feet, while Nona dozed. She would waken abruptly and tell Linn a story, then nod off again. She had died when Linn was ten.

"I know Pele. I'm not like her, you are right."

Linn supposed she shouldn't be surprised that Granny Clinch knew Pele. The immortals were a small community, she was discovering. "I wanted to ask why you seem so ordinary, if you are immortal."

"I've been Granny for so long, child, they all know me as this, and just this. By being ordinary, they forget just how long Granny has been..."

Linn told her, "I teased Bes into youthening."

Granny cackled. "Bes is a good-for-nothing with a wicked sense of humor. You tell him I said that."

Linn smiled, then frowned. "I don't know where he went. He left us at Mac'Lir's castle without a goodbye."

Granny stopped laughing. "Here and I have been wasting time with stories. Bes left you alone when you were in his charge?"

"Well, I'm not a child." Linn objected. "I'm sure he was just called away by an emergency," she added with a surge of loyalty.

"And who else was in your retinue?"

"Retinue?" Linn echoed, confused.

"The group sent by your grandfather. I've been remembering the past too much." Granny reached out and patted Linn on the head.

"Well, me, and Blackie, and Spot... that's Blackie's brother. And Deirdre. Spot stayed with Deirdre, because she wasn't ready for an adventure."

"Is she younger than you?" Granny asked.

"Yes, a little. Spot and Blackie are only two, but, well..." Linn looked toward the house. Blackie hadn't come back yet.

"God's children develop differently." Granny nodded wisely. "None of mine had enough god's blood to show."

Linn got back up and went to her chair. "So, we were all old enough to look after ourselves, you see."

They could hear running steps coming through the house, and all three of them stood up. Linn and Merrick were at the door ahead of Granny, who was spry, but no match for their youthful enthusiasm. Blackie burst through the door and grabbed Linn.

"We have to go! Something's wrong with Spot."

"What?" Linn was confused. How would he know?

"Wait a moment." Granny Clinch took his shoulder. "Don't go off half-cocked, boy. You can't possibly get there fast enough to make a difference. Now, what do you know?"

"I don't get anything like clear words or pictures from him, you know." Blackie's speech was so fast it was slurred. "Just that he's in danger, and afraid for Dee..."

"Dee?" Granny asked.

"Deirdre, the coblyn girl." Linn supplied, since Blackie appeared to have lost the ability to speak entirely.

"She's a coblyn?" Granny let go of Blackie's shoulder, and he started to pace.

"Yes, didn't I say?" Having Granny Clinch in your face, Linn was discovering, was a scary experience. Her eyes were remarkably sharp and piercing, like she could see inside your head.

"No, you didn't. Coblyns mature very slowly compared to humans. She may seem your age, but she is still a child. Blackie." Granny reached out and caught his hand. He came to a halt, quivering slightly.

"Yes'm," he responded miserably.

"What was your brother's impression of the danger?"

"Under attack..." Blackie shivered. "Little people, like Dee."

"Little people attacking right after Mac'Lir's return? I think I know what you will face. It won't be pretty. Perhaps you should wait, while we call for help."

"No!" all three of the young people spoke at once. Granny looked from face to face.

"You don't know what you are facing," She pointed out gently.

"These are our friends," Linn started.

Merrick interjected, "and family. We need to go now, please."

"Bes may have been lured away. I think you will find that a goblin swarm attacked the castle, hoping to catch Mac'Lir weak and vulnerable before he called all his people back together again." Granny patted Blackie's hand and let go of it.

"If you insist on going, use your strengths, children. Don't lose your heads and jump right into the fire."

Linn closed her eyes and tried to think. She had Lambent, tucked away like Pele had shown her, along with her backpack. And her cell phone. Her eyes popped open. She focused her power, and reached for the backpack, pulling it out of the place between where it had been stashed. Merrick was a sight, as he startled sideways and his eyes widened.

Granny nodded. "Good girl. Now, boy, your family has never fought alone, and although there are no wolves in Kentucky..."

Merrick nodded thoughtfully. "I should go outside first."

"Please do," the old lady said drily.

As he walked through the door, she turned to Blackie. "I have a gift for you."

"Oh, I couldn't accept..." he started. Linn turned on him.

"Shush! In the fairy tales, the real ones, not the silly happy birdy ones, when the old woman offers help and gifts to the hero, he has to treat her with respect and take it, because it's important."

Granny Clinch laughed out loud at this. "Mythology has taken the shapes it has, in stories and legends, for a reason, child. I don't say you are wrong. Come with me, Blackie."

Linn was left alone, with the peaceful valley full of birdsong below her, and she turned on her cell phone. A truly modern weapon, she thought, amusing herself. She had a bar of signal. It flickered away, then came back. She tried walking around, which didn't help.

Linn made the call; not sure it would go through.

"Mom?"

Theta's voice sounded warped. "Linn? Is everything all right? Bes arrived here, but we hadn't called him. He's on his way back to you."

"We're not with Mac'Lir..." Linn started. The phone emitted a warble, and the call dropped. She looked at the screen. No service bars.

Linn went into the house, not seeing Blackie and Granny Clinch, so she went all the way outside. There, she stopped in the open door in surprise. Merrick was standing in the yard, eyes closed, and a ring of creatures around him.

A regal German Shepherd dog got up and trotted over to her. He sat in front of her and looked up, then offered his paw, gravely. Linn shook it, feeling silly.

Merrick spoke. "I'm calling to the wolves, and he will be your bodyguard."

"Does he have a name?" Linn asked. "Or are you controlling him?"

"Oh, um, I don't know, and I'm not really controlling that one, he's very well trained already. Just enhancing his intelligence a little."

Linn looked down at the bright brown eyes. "I shall call you Colonel," she murmured to the dog. She looked back at Merrick.

He had dogs and coyotes, and something that looked an awful lot like a wolf. She could count twenty... twenty-one with the Colonel who was pacing beside her now in perfect heel position.

"How many can you handle?"

Linn was familiar with the concept from Coyote, who could send a bit of his Power with an animal to use as a mobile spy.

"I think this is as much as I can. I haven't done this by myself before. I have a headache." He rubbed his temples.

"Are you going to be ok?" Linn didn't know how she could help, but she could try.

"Yeah. It's just that one..." Merrick glared at the wolf, who lolled out a pink tongue in a doggy laugh. "He's fighting me."

"How did you find a wolf?"

"Oh, he's a wolf-dog. It was fashionable a while back. People didn't realize how hard they were to train, and a lot of them wound up abandoned."

Linn looked down at the beautiful dog next to her. "Surely he wasn't abandoned."

Merrick shook his head. "Most of them aren't. I will have to make sure they can get back home, after..."

He looked sick with worry, now.

"We'll leave as soon as Blackie is ready." Linn assured him. She looked at her phone. Still no signal, drat. She powered it off. It didn't work in the Path, or the other plane.

They were alone, and facing an unknown enemy. "Merrick, can you guide the Path?"

He looked dubious. "I don't think so."

"The only place I know how to go is the castle itself, which might land us in the middle of the trouble, or that farm where you rescued me." Linn mused.

He looked alarmed. "That's on earth."

"And it won't help." She sighed and shook her head. "It's miles from the doorway to the *sidhe*."

"I can help with the location to guide you to." Granny Clinch walked out of the house, Blackie on her heels.

"Are you coming with us?" Linn felt her heart leap. Oddly, for all that she was trying to be grown up, the idea of having an adult to lean on was very reassuring.

Granny shook her head. "No, child, I cannot leave here."

Granny held out her hands, and Linn grasped them. Granny closed her eyes, and Linn followed her lead. With the sight, she could see Granny's green aura, the clear green of grass, rather than Mac'Lir's stormy gray-green. A spark leapt from Granny to Linn, and she could feel the jolt of it, like a big fat static electricity shock.

"Ooh..." Linn rubbed her hands together, as Granny released them.

"You will do well, girl." Granny hugged her, and Linn leaned into the old woman, feeling how she was bones and sinew, small where she looked bigger than she really was through force of personality.

Blackie had shifted back to cat form, and now he walked over and shouldered into Linn.

"Can you talk in this form?" She asked him.

He yawned, revealing his long fangs and pink tongue. Linn took that as a no.

"We will be back to return the dogs," she told Granny, and opened the High Path.

There was a moment of confusion as Merrick rallied his pack through and into the dimensional rift. Linn stepped calmly into it, and the Colonel walked beside her without hesitation. She took a deep breath, and tried to steady her racing heart.

They might not be much, but they could at least try. She started to run.

10

BATTLEFIELD

*L*inn stepped out of the High Path into a world of swirling mist. The grass under her feet was pearled with dew-drops, and she couldn't see far at all. This wasn't a natural fog; she knew at once. She had been part of a party moving under the cover of a sea-fog like this once before. Only they hadn't been attacking, just being very, very secretive.

Now, she listened. The world was hushed, closed in to the area surrounding her like a soft cocoon. Linn whistled softly. Merrick, his pack at his heels, stepped out of the path, with Blackie taking the rear position. They paused for a second, like her, orienting themselves. The Colonel licked her hand, making Linn jump.

Then the whole pack turned like one, ears pricking forward, and she could hear it too. The clash of metal, and hoarse shouts. They surged forward, Merrick shifting as they began to ran, and all the beasts were gone into the fog, leaving her alone with the big shepherd. She looked down at him and sighed.

"I need to be faster. Or a horse. A horse would be good."

None appeared out of the fog, so she started to jog in the direction the pack had gone. She didn't dare break into a full run. First, arriving where the fight was worn out and out of breath would be a bad thing. Second, stepping in a gopher hole or on a rock and breaking an ankle would just be humiliating.

This would be the second time she would arrive on the battlefield. The first time the fighting had all been over, and a truce for healing called between combatants. She had had no idea what had happened, or where they were. This felt eerily like that, only now the fighting was still going on.

"So, this is what they mean about the fog of war," she commented to the Colonel, who was ranging ahead, then behind, in a sort of ellipse that had her at the focus. "No one knows what the hell is going on."

The swear word, however mild, made her feel both guilty and weirdly grown up. "I think I want-"

Linn reached up over her shoulder and pulled Lambent from the portal without breaking her stride. The sword's blade coruscated with light, a display of the power pent up when it was created and dedicated to her. Linn really wanted a pistol, and her rifle, and maybe a shotgun... no, definitely a shotgun, one of the kinds with a magazine. That wasn't possible. Lambent would have to do, and the light was pushing the fog away from them.

It wasn't until she paid attention to the effect her sword was having on the fog that Linn realized what it had been doing. Tendrils of it had been reaching toward her, like fingers. Now, they flinched back sharply, retreating into the bank of white cloud stuff. She held Lambent in front of her, never stopping, moving onward, the big dog staying behind her now, guarding where she couldn't see. Linn moved slowly, listening.

A yelp off to the left a bit sounded like one of Merrick's pack. She shifted her direction toward it. The fog retreated, and she could see a yellowish-brown coyote rolling in combat with a small creature she couldn't make out well. They were moving quickly enough she didn't dare stab at it, lest she hit the pack animal and injure it, by extension injuring Merrick as well.

Linn lowered Lambent as they rolled toward her, and poked sharply when a bony back was topmost. The thing shrilled, and let go of the coyote. It had been clamped on with legs and arms, biting at the thickly furred neck with teeth and not making much headway, Linn realized in the split second as it stood up, because there wasn't a lot of blood on its mouth. Now, it began to dance around, trying to reach the wound on its back with both hands and making pitiful noises.

Linn hesitated. It had to be a goblin. She could see the resemblance to the coblyns, but where they were well-formed and even beautiful, this warped thing was something from a deep nightmare. Greenish-brown, streaked with filth, and with only a few wisps of hair on an over-large head, it wailed one last time, and then turned on her. She held up Lambent as it leapt, wide black eyes gleaming in the reflected light, mouth gaping hideously and showing jagged, broken teeth. The Colonel hit it in midair, with a sickening crunch and snap of his jaws, and they both landed in a heap to her right. Linn took a step back.

The dog shook itself, glanced at her, and paced around behind her again. Linn swallowed hard, trying not to look at the crumpled body of the goblin, and started moving again. She could hear barks and screams, now, and a hoarse roaring that made her shiver. With Lambent held loosely in front of her, so her arms weren't under too much strain, she trotted toward the battle.

The ground began to drop away under her, and she stumbled, afraid she would fall. As she straightened, Lambent at her side, there was a flash of green light, like all the lightning bolts in the world hitting something in front of her, and she stopped, dazzled and half-blind for a second. When her eyesight cleared, she could see that the fog was gone, and the battlefield stretched out before her. It backed up against the castle, and she could see a knot of people in the gate, fighting, and all across the garden were goblins, beasts she didn't recognize, and Merrick's pack, snarling and howling. The deep roar sounded again, to her left, and her head snapped around. Blackie, rearing, his mouth open and red, screaming a roar, his war-cry, as a wave of goblins attacked him.

Linn lifted Lambent high and started running. She trusted the Colonel, and the coyote he seemed to have deputized, to cover her back. She kept an eye on her destination, but tried to look everywhere else, too. This time, when the goblin popped up like a jack-in-the-box, she didn't hesitate, simply swung Lambent while continuing her own momentum, and the sharp-edged sword bit into his neck. She jerked the blade free, feeling it grate on bone, and out of the corner of her eye she could see the Colonel snap a goblin neck like he was shaking a rag doll. She didn't stop. She couldn't stop.

She became aware that she was screaming, her voice raw. Lambent was dripping with blood, as she hacked inelegantly at two goblins attacking her. One held a kitchen knife, the other a corroded, broken shard of a sword. She cut through the wrist that held it, and it tumbled to the trampled herbs they were running through. She didn't dare stop moving. Blackie's coughing roar came again, as he dropped the goblin whose throat he had just ripped out in a spray of blood, and she caught his eye.

They didn't need to talk. They had fought like this once before, with less light than the leaden sky overhead let fall. Back-to-back, turning slowly, they moved toward the gate, letting the goblins come to them. The coyote and the Colonel made up the other points of their compass, and Linn stopped thinking about it... There wasn't time, between one goblin on the point of her sword, and the next leaping at her legs, trying to bit through her Achilles tendon. She saw abstractly that some of the blood running down her leg now wasn't goblin green, but she didn't feel the pain. There wasn't time. She had to keep moving.

The castle wall, rough, gray stone, with windows high above them, came up suddenly. She hadn't been looking at it, only at what was moving in front of her. They had been joined by another two of Merrick's dogs, and the gate wasn't far. The wall meant they could put their backs to it and move slowly sideways, hacking and hewing and biting, always toward the gate. Linn watched another green lightning bolt reach out, flickering, horizontal... someone at the gate had a powerful weapon.

There was something here that wasn't a goblin. It turned away from the gate it was attacking, looming over them, a small figure Linn couldn't make out in its huge hand. The troll dropped the little creature, Linn was very afraid it was a coblyn, and couldn't look... and reached out for her. Merrick, in wolf-form, barking like mad, flung himself on the massive forearm. White teeth flashed as Merrick slashed with them at the tendons in the wrist. The troll howled with rage and pain, and with tears in the tiny eyes, tried to curl up around the painful wound.

Linn charged. As the troll drew his arm up toward his chest, taking Merrick for a ride, she slashed at the closest inner thigh, hoping that it was as delicate an area on a troll as it was on a human. She left a gaping wound in the wake of her blade, the clear blood sizzling with the power she was channeling. The troll dropped to his knees, keening on a scale that raised the hair on the back of her neck. Merrick howled and fell free of the troll. He was rubbing his head on the ground now, and Linn realized that the troll's screams were above human hearing range and into a range that hurt the wolf's ears.

"Merrick!" she shouted, hoping he could hear her. "Shift! Shift!"

She couldn't stop to see if he did. The troll's throat, since he was on his knees now, was almost in reach. Holding Lambent with both hands, and channeling enough power to make it look like the blade was on fire, she leapt toward the unguarded head of the troll, who was supporting himself on his knuckles. Her blade sank in deep beneath his chin, and the clear blood spurted out, splashing over her and burning. Linn realized with horror that troll's blood was acid. He fell forward, as her momentum carried her up, and she kicked off his upper arm and used her free hand on the back of his neck to get herself up onto his back and he collapsed flat, driving Lambent all the way through his spine. Linn had let go of her sword in the mad scramble to stay on top, and she stood on his back, screaming. She couldn't help it. The wounds earlier hadn't hurt, but the troll blood burned and she couldn't move, couldn't think–

A wave of gray-green washed over her, and she felt her eyes roll back in her head. The sounds faded out, and her knees buckled.

Linn woke up staring at grayness, backlit, and painful to her eyes, which burned. She tried to lift a hand to rub them, and discovered that she couldn't move. She was bound in some way. With a squeak of alarm, she tried to wriggle free, feeling her skin itch and crawl. Whimpering, she had to stop to take a breath, and the Colonel's fuzzy face appeared in her line of sight. He looked at her with big, liquid puppy-dog eyes, and licked his nose. Linn made herself relax. She might be tied up, but the dog wasn't worried, which hopefully meant she shouldn't be, either.

Relaxing didn't help the pain. Her upper body, throat, and face burned like she had poison ivy and a sunburn all at once, and she couldn't touch anything, her hands were immobilized. It didn't feel like ropes, just that she was held down by something soft.

"Colonel, are you sitting on me?" Linn rasped. Her own voice startled her, husky and raspy. Her throat ached. How much screaming had she been doing? Was the battle over? She turned her head away from the big dog, who blocked her view on that side, and discovered she was lying very near the vast bulk of the troll, who wasn't moving. Linn looked up at the sky again. The sun was starting to burn through the clouds, and tears started streaming from her eyes in pain as the light hurt them. She closed her eyes.

Not being able to move made her think about how much she hurt. Her leg, where the goblin had gotten under her guard and taken a chunk out. It couldn't have been too bad; she was able to keep running on it. Her upper body, which itched and burned. The troll's blood hadn't been hydrochloric acid, or she'd be dying in agony. But it hadn't been lemon juice, either. Linn shivered. The Colonel nosed her cheek and stretched his body out alongside hers, offering her some welcome warmth.

She started thinking about the battle, what she could have done differently, done better. There had been no way to know about the danger of the troll blood, but could she have struck differently to keep her sword? A slashing blow rather than a stab would have been the ticket. Linn twitched. She still couldn't move, and didn't know why.

Images she hadn't really processed during the heat of battle came back now, flashing into her mind. The broken body of one of the dogs, tripping her and feeling slippery under her feet where it- Linn tried to think about something, anything else. Had they won? Where were Merrick and Blackie now?

She got images she wasn't entirely sure were right, of Blackie under a pile of goblins, still fighting. Had she seen that, or was her imagination creating her worst fears? She knew she had seen a coblyn fall, broken, from the troll's grasp. She had refused to look, then, as it might have been Deirdre. Now, the body falling limply, cartwheeling in midair, kept replaying behind her eyelids. Linn opened her eyes.

The tears started again instantly, and this time it wasn't all pain causing them. Or not the pain of damage, anyway. A fuzzy image loomed into her range of vision, and she flinched. It disappeared again, and then a blobby face surrounded by dark fuzz appeared.

"Linn? Linn, honey, can you see me?" Her mother's voice was the sweetest thing Linn had ever heard.

Linn opened her mouth, but all that would come out was a croak.

"Oh, sweetie..." The shape that was her mother moved away, then back. Linn felt the bite valve of a camelback. She sucked greedily. Her mouth tasted vile, full of stuff she didn't want to think about, and the water was sweet and delicious. She had to stop for breath a couple of times, but her mother didn't take it away until Linn pushed it out of her mouth.

"Mom! When did you get here?"

"In just about enough time to see you doing a victory dance atop a huge troll, and then Mac'Lir wrapped you in a spell to keep you from further harm."

Her mother sounded equal parts amused and scared.

"I'm sorry..."

"Oh, baby. You need to lie still and rest... We're working all over on healing spells; sorry we didn't get to you sooner." Linn felt her mother's hand on hers, squeezing gently. It was sore, but not too bad. The other one had taken the worst of the blood, and throbbed abominably.

Theta murmured and Linn could see the glow of her power through closed eyes. A deep sleep sucked her down into utter blackness, and she was glad the images couldn't follow her, until she was too soundly unconscious to care any longer.

11

RECOVERY

*L*inn woke up in a bed. She lay there for a long time, assessing how she felt, and a bit afraid to open her eyes. She ached all over, but the burning and itching seemed to have gone away. She flexed the hand that had been drenched in acid. It worked. Linn opened her eyes and blinked.

They felt crusty and like someone had poured sand in them, but she could see clearly again. The ceiling overhead, rough plaster and age-blackened beams, was familiar. She turned her head, and saw Deirdre sitting in the chair reading. Deja vu.

"Hello." Linn's throat felt much better, and that actually sounded like a word, not something a frog would say.

She was enormously relieved to see her friend, whole and apparently healthy. "Where are Merrick and Blackie?"

Deirdre was getting a glass of water for her. "They are fine. Being healed, like you."

Linn levered herself up on her elbows and took the glass once she was sitting. "I feel much better."

Dee snorted. "You should, you've been asleep for three days."

Linn choked on her water. Dee took the glass before she made more of a mess, and patted her back while she regained the ability to breathe.

"Three days?" Then she remembered something else. "My mom?"

"She's here. Want me to go get her?"

Linn nodded. "And Spot, is he ok?"

Dee nodded. "He was with me. He's mad he missed the fighting."

Linn smiled wryly. "Boys!"

She could hear Deirdre laughing as she walked down the hall. Linn lay back and started at the ceiling, not seeing it, but rather the face of Granny Clinch, telling them stories about Manannan Mac'Lir. That had only been the beginning, Linn knew now. There was something coming, and with the goblin attack, she was afraid it might be bigger than she could handle.

On the other hand, she had started this, she really wanted to finish it. There were so many things she didn't know... didn't need to know, really, as much as she was dying of curiosity some days. This situation, with Mac'Lir, she knew there was a lot unseen, things she could only guess at. The battle made her shiver, thinking about it now. At the time, she'd just stopped thinking and done.

Theta walked into her room and came to sit on the side of the bed. "How do you feel, baby?"

Linn sat up, which came easier than it had the first time. "I'm okay... a lot better than I was." She wrinkled her nose, remembering the pain and stink of the dead troll and other things, lying there.

"I was so scared for you." Her mother touched her cheek gently. "I'd like to take you home, to Sanctuary, if you feel up to traveling today."

Linn swallowed, hard, and blinked back tears. It took her a fraction of a second to make her decision, and a lot longer to tell her mother. "I... I have a job to do, still. If Mac'Lir will trust me." She wasn't sure about that part. She hadn't been able to report on the first trip, yet. Mac'Lir had been in the gate, but she was not yet to him when the troll had charged... Linn shuddered.

"Linnea..." Theta started, then stopped. Linn could see she was thinking. "You're growing up," Theta finally added softly.

Linn nodded.

Another set of footsteps clattered along the hall, stopping at Linn's door. Theta looked around as the unseen person rapped on the open door, and cleared their throat.

"Lady Vulkane, Mac'Lir would like audience with your daughter, if she is awake?"

Theta stood and Linn could see that the coblyn who was in the doorway was unfamiliar. He wore bandages, so he must have been involved in the fighting. On second glance, she didn't think he was actually a coblyn, either. He was the right size, but tanned rather than greenish, and with small, rounded ears. His thick brown hair looked as though he had run his fingers through it, as it stood on end.

"I think I can get up," Linn told her mother. The little being in the doorway beamed at her.

"So good to see you on the mend, Miss." His cheerful voice was at odds with the amount of white gauze she could see. There might be more, but he was wearing long pants, boots, and a short-sleeved white shirt. "I'm Dugan, you can call me Dug. Bein's as we fought together."

"We did?" Linn was sure she would remember him, and she couldn't.

"Well, manner of speakin' as you were on one side of the troll and I was on t'other. Thing of beauty, that sword thrust and leap." He shook his head, still smiling in admiration. Linn peeked under her blankets. She seemed to be wearing a long dress-nightgown, and nothing else.

"Um, Dug? Could you give me a minute?" She was sure she shouldn't attend the king's summons in her nightie.

The cheerful little man swung the door shut, and Linn stood up with her mother hovering. She wobbled a little, once on her feet, but it didn't hurt any more than lying down had.

"Oh, dear. I'm not sure where my clothes are..." Linn looked in vain.

"You couldn't have worn those. The acid destroyed most of the fabric, and we had to cut the rest off." Her mother sounded upset again.

"I have a change in my backpack." Linn started to pull it out of the space pocket where it had been since she left Granny Clinch's house.

"I think you should wear that." Her mother pointed at a rack behind the door. It had been hidden before, but now Linn could see the fabric hanging there. Closer inspection revealed a long yellow dress embroidered beautifully with red and orange birds, and a white thin dress like the one she was wearing.

With Theta's help, Linn got dressed. It turned out the thin white fabric dress was an under-thing, and the stiff outer one laced up. Even the long sleeves laced on. Linn looked down at herself. "This is positively medieval."

Theta laughed. "That's because it is. I have noticed since my arrival that time seems to have stopped, here."

"We're not on earth, I know that much." Linn found the shoes were very comfortable, but more like soft moccasins. It was when she bent over to put them on that she made a discovery.

"My hair!" Linn put her hands to her head, finding short, feathery hair on one side, above her ears, and on the other, it fell to her shoulder. "What happened?" she wailed, sitting back on the bed and wanting a mirror badly.

"Shh..." Theta sat next to her and wrapped an arm around her gently. "We had to cut it – and you will want to have it styled again when we get home – the acid blood ate through your braid. It looked and smelled horrible."

Linn watched her mother wrinkle her nose in memory. Now she thought she could remember that burning-smell hair odor, but there had been so much else going on.

Dug rapped on the door. "Everything all right in there?"

"Yes," Theta called back. "We're coming now."

Linn nodded. It was silly to be worried about her hair at a time like this. It was just... she had never had short hair. She touched the ragged ends again as her mother opened the door. Walking down the hall, she felt off balance. It wasn't just the loss of her hair's familiar weight; it was how much had happened in only two days. She didn't feel the same, but everything still looked the same.

As they approached the Great Hall, where the doors were closed, Linn saw Deirdre had dressed in a pretty gown in the same style as hers. Only Dee's was dark green, which somehow made her skin look just pale. Spot was sitting erect next to her, his sleek tail wrapped neatly around his paws. Dugan opened the doors with a flourish, and Deirdre and Spot followed Linn and her mother into the hall, Dugan staying with the doors.

Mac'Lir was sitting on his throne, looking grey and grim. He had a patch of gauze on his forehead with very modern medical tape, which looked terribly incongruous in the setting of the ancient castle. Linn tried not to stare at it.

"Lady Vulkane, Daughter of Fire." Mac'Lir greeted them. He sounded tired and sad. "Daughter of Fire, are you well?"

Linn felt oddly shy. Before, she hadn't been reverent of him at all, but now... he looked like the old king he had been. "I am healing, I think."

"Can you relate your adventure to our Court?" He asked gently, leaning forward and stretching out a hand to her.

Hesitantly, she stepped up on to the low dais and at a slight gesture from him, turned to face the Hall. There weren't many people there, and she knew half of them, so she relaxed slightly, and started to tell the story. It didn't take her long to discover that she couldn't look at her mother. Theta's emotions showed so clearly on her face, it upset Linn to see her reacting to the idea of her daughter being threatened with a gun and then tied up.

At the end of her tale, she looked at the king. "We failed; I know. We didn't check the call out before I knocked, and... And we had to be rescued."

To her surprise, Mac'Lir chuckled. "Daughter of Fire, you are too modest." He reached over to the low table beside his throne, overflowing with papers, books, and parchments. A roll of parchment was flourished in front of her. "An old friend sent me her assessment of the three young people who had visited her. Along with it, a chastisement of me for being too hasty and endangering them without a full understanding of the call that was being sent out by rote."

"Oh." Linn could just imagine how Granny Clinch had said it, too.

"In addition, there is the act that you, all three of you, returned with a distress call and plunged into battle on my side without a hesitation. Can you still say that I have not seen your true mettle?"

Linn shook her head, mutely.

Mac'Lir went on, his mirth dropping away, and lowering the scroll to his lap. "What comes now is more uncertain, and you, I have learned, are perhaps the most able of all the elder blood to carry it out."

Linn blinked in surprise. "Me? I'm not special..."

He shook his head. "I hate to ask this of you, so soon after you were injured grievously in battle alongside me. There are forces you do not know of at play, and I have been too much out of the world below to keep track of them, myself. The goblin raid was only a raid. There will be others, in search of my secrets, and I must keep the raiders from them. However, this is only possible with your help."

He leaned forward, and Linn faced him, everyone else in the room forgotten as she listened intently to the king. "Are you willing to quest on my behalf once more? I cannot give you time to rest and heal; this must be done quickly."

Linn nodded. "I had already wanted to continue with my mission. Mom asked me if I would come home, but..." She spread her hands, helplessly trying to find the words for feeling responsible to finish this. It sounded pompous and silly in her head.

He nodded. "I understand."

Linn could see in his stormy grey eyes that he did. Mac'Lir smiled just a little at her. "I look forward to you meeting my daughter."

He leaned back in his throne and raised his voice enough for the whole room to hear. "Linnea, Daughter of Fire, on the second eve, you will go forth with a band of chosen companions. You will have all I can render to aid you on your way, and the security of my kingdom, nay, an entire world, rests on your quest. Do you accept?"

Linn took a deep breath. She didn't think he was putting her on, with that save the world bit. And he hadn't told her why he thought she was special. But she couldn't back down now. "Yes, I do."

"Then we will meet on the morrow, for planning. Until then, rest, feast, and be merry with your compatriots!" He finished with a flourish, and Linn stepped back off the platform and her mother took her arm when she wobbled a little on landing.

"Come on, let's put you back in bed." Theta didn't talk more until they were out in the hall, Deirdre and Spot silently tagging along.

"Mom..." Linn wasn't sure what to say. I don't have a driver's license yet, but I'm needed to save the world?

"You will always be my little girl." Theta had Linn's hand tucked in the crook of her arm, and she pressed it gently. "But you are growing up, and I have to let go. You are special, my dear girl."

"How am I special?" Linn was starting to feel a bit cranky about that. She didn't feel any different, really. Just off balance from the last couple of days. Nothing major had changed.

Her mother didn't get a chance to answer before Blackie and Merrick came around the corner. Blackie was back to cat-form. They stopped dead and stared at the women. Merrick's jaw dropped.

"Linn?" He asked, his voice breaking.

Linn looked at them. It was hard to tell, with Blackie, if he'd been hurt. Merrick had a bandage on one hand, but seemed to be healthy otherwise.

"What, have I turned into a monster?" She was already cranky, snapping at them came naturally.

Merrick turned bright red, and Blackie lay down flat on the hall floor, turning his head so he wasn't looking at her. Linn felt her own jaw drop. "Mo-om!" She wailed, turning and grabbing her mother's arm with both hands "I need a mirror!"

It turned out there were very few mirrors in the old castle. Deirdre, not meeting Linn's angry glances – why hadn't she said anything? – led her to a full-length one in an unused and very beautiful bedroom. Linn stood and looked into it for a long couple of moments, and then took a deep breath.

"It's ok." she reassured her friends. "I just..." her voice wobbled. "I just will have to learn how to wear make-up."

12

HAIRCUT

*H*er mother shook her head, "No, what you need is some time in the sun again. The discoloration isn't permanent, it's just that your new skin isn't tanned and the old skin is."

"Oh." Linn looked back into the mirror, taking a little longer now. "It's not so bad, then. But my hair..." She touched the longer side mournfully.

"I know who can cut it neatly for you," Deirdre offered.

The boys, who were all three hovering in the doorway, bumping into one another, were Linn's next target. "And you guys – you gave me a heart attack!"

"Didn't mean to!" Merrick spoke for them. "It was just... I didn't expect..."

Linn sighed. "I wonder if there's any soda and pizza on this plane."

Her mother laughed out loud. "I don't think so." Theta looked at all of them. "But I think it would be good for the five of you to have a little party. I will see what I can come up with. Deirdre, can you find a place for you chi-" Theta corrected herself, "You young people to hang out in?"

"Well, there's the library..."

All three boys groaned. Dee grinned, showing her sharp teeth. "Now, it's not just because I love books! There's a table, and comfy chairs, and something I want to show Linn. But you might be interested in goblin history, too."

"That might be interesting," Merrick admitted reluctantly.

They reassembled less than an hour later in the library. Linn had wanted her spare clothes rather than the long gown, and Blackie walked in on two legs, which visibly startled Dee and Spot. Spot looked at his brother, then down at his own paws.

"I want to be able to talk..." Blackie explained. He was still wearing the nice clothes he'd appeared in at Granny's house. Linn thought he looked spiffy, and told him so. She'd also discovered that making her friend blush was a lot of fun.

Deirdre, giggling, disappeared into the disheveled stacks. Linn looked around. She hadn't really been paying attention when she'd visited the library before, only wanting something to read. She'd had an impression of controlled chaos, which she now revised.

It was sheer chaos. Everything was random, piles teetered on top of shelves. There were piles of flat stones under the narrow window. Everything was dusty, like it hadn't been touched in ages. Linn peered at the stones, which had deep runic scratches on them. As old as some of this was – literally ages, not just years – Hypatia would love it.

Deirdre reappeared, a huge book in her arms. The pages seemed to be falling out.

"Hey! Here..." Blackie jumped forward and swept a lot of the papers from a section of the table so the tiny girl could set it down.

"Careful!" she chided him. "Some of that is very delicate!"

"Well, you were about to drop that thing," he pointed out reasonably.

"This thing," Deirdre opened the cover reverently, "is the closest I have been able to find to a compiled history of the coblyn and goblin lines."

"I know you told me, or your uncle did, in class, that Coblyns and Goblins were all the same, until a point when your family emigrated, and the ones who stayed behind... changed." Linn could remember that first creature, fighting with the coyote, and then attacking her. Which reminded her...

"Merrick, the dogs? Your pack?"

He ducked his head and rubbed the back of his neck with one hand. "I lost three of them. The rest are safely back where they came from."

"The Colonel?" Linn asked, a little pang of worry for the dog hitting her.

"What?" he looked confused.

Linn realized she'd only named the dog after they were separated. "The big shepherd you assigned to me."

"Oh, yeah. Tough boy. He was fine, just scratches. Wouldn't leave your side until you were tucked into bed, actually." Merrick smiled, and Linn smiled back. She had liked the big dog, and had come to appreciate Merrick's motivation in assigning her a bodyguard.

"Ahem." Deirdre said, not at all subtly. "Goblins?"

"Yeah, what about 'em?" Merrick straddled a chair backwards and rested his folded arms on it. "I know we've had little skirmishes. Some nasty incidents." He frowned hard. "Da used to tell stories, but it was silly stuff. And Uncle Lem... he flew in the war, and used to tell me stories, but Mam made him stop when I couldn't sleep after one."

"Mothers are spoilsports." Linn said, as Theta walked in with an enormous tray of food.

She laughed. "Oh, what have I done now? Interrupted something?"

Linn jumped up from the stack of stones she was sitting on. "No, not you! Only Merrick's Mom, who wouldn't let his uncle tell him stories that gave him nightmares."

Theta blinked. "Well, I think that sounds practical, actually." She looked at the table. "Is there a place to put this?"

It took a couple of minutes and a flurry of papers for the teens to clear the loose papers off the table. They left the big book of goblin history in place. Bronwyn came in with a basket of glasses and a pitcher of something.

"A picnic in the library!" she said cheerfully. "Now, this is a first. Of course, the garden isn't fit for it right now."

"Oh, dear, the beautiful garden." Linn said, taking a glass of the iced tea. She sipped and then looked into the glass. "This is... interesting."

"Your mother showed me how to make that." Bronwyn beamed. "I never thought of drinking tea cold. Added a bit of honey and lemon, and it's right tasty."

Linn nodded and deliberately took another very slow sip. "Thank you." She told the little brown lady. "Are you any relation to Dugan?" She asked. There was a strong resemblance.

"Oh, heavens no. Only that we're both Brownies, you know." Bronwyn looked at the spread and then went out again, her skirts swishing.

"Brownies?" Linn looked at Merrick and Deirdre. "There are so many people I had no idea..."

"Brownies are connected to coblyns and goblins. All the little people are descended from the same people. I don't know quite why they..." Dee spread her hands apart, indicating distances.

"I don't think that's as important as the beginning." Linn had a feeling. She had always wondered where the coblyns came from. If her ancestors had come through from another universe, where had they come from? They certainly weren't human.

"Well, the histories are more about the coblyns. I don't precisely know why the goblins are so angry at us, and the king." Deirdre leaned over the book, carefully turning pages. "They don't seem to write, you see."

"Not at all?" Blackie sounded scandalized, and Linn grinned at him.

"You don't write, either. I think I just figured out why you prefer to be a cat."

He stuck his tongue out at her, and Theta laughed. "I'm going to leave you lot to squabble amongst yourselves. If you want anything..." She got up and rubbed her behind. "Those stones are hard! If you want anything, you're big enough to get it yourselves!" Theta sailed out the door, laughing.

Merrick looked at Linn, smiling. "Your mom is fun."

"Yes, she is. She lets me get away with a lot, but not too much."

Deirdre had a mouthful of pasty, which were evidently Bronwyn's answer to pizza. She swallowed. "I didn't say they didn't write at all."

Linn was used to her friend's tenacity when it was a topic she wanted to discuss to the bitter end. "What did they write, then?"

"I'm surprised they could write." Merrick growled. He glared at his pasty and then bit into it fiercely.

Linn sighed, her mind's eye supplying her with plenty of reasons why he had that idea. The goblin gnawing at her leg, his eyes empty of any intelligence, only animal hunger. Linn rubbed her leg, feeling the sore patch where the bite had sunk in. Her mother's healing had knitted the torn muscles, but full healing would take some time.

Deirdre crowed. "Here it is!"

The page in question was evidently not bound in, as she lifted it right out of the book. From the ragged edges, Linn didn't think it had ever been. Deirdre walked over to the window, where Linn was perched on the stones again.

"It's very faint, I need the light." Dee explained, and Linn wiggled over to give her more. The pasty she was munching had been filled with cheese and sausage and was quite good. It was not helped as she got a whiff of the page Dee was holding.

"Whew! What is that smell?" Linn leaned away from her friend.

Merrick growled. "You don't recognize it? It's eau d'goblin. I reeked after the fighting."

"What is that, written in blood?" The ink looked greenish.

"Wouldn't surprise me." Blackie came and leaned over Deirdre's shoulder. "I can't make heads or tails of that, Dee. What does it say?"

"I haven't been able to make much of it out. That, and I think a lot of it is the same thing, repeated over and over. 'Slaves, dogs, and dirt-nosers.'"

"Talking about goblins?" Linn asked. They certainly had seemed dirty.

"No, this is addressed to my great-great something great-grandfather. The goblins hate the coblyns. They think we sold out our race and chose to be, as this accuses, slaves." Dee took the page back to the book and wiped her hands before picking up more food.

"So that is why they are attacking Mac'Lir?" Blackie sounded as mystified as Linn felt, although she would have said it with less food in her mouth.

"Well..." Deirdre curled up in one of the chairs, tucking her feet under her. "You know my line, the coblyns, left the caves and mines where we had dwelt for time immemorial. We were not slaves or servants to anyone, but the cadet branch, the Brownies, chose to assist the farmers. We were allied with the miners, and came to the New

World with them, and in time, to Sanctuary, but that was after... other things."

Linn remembered Deirdre telling her of a girlhood in the castle, and she didn't know how old Sanctuary was, really. So many secrets. She sighed. Dee kept talking.

"The goblins were a few families, one clan, who chose to remain behind, in abandoned tunnels and mines, and they went very strange."

"I'll say!" Merrick exclaimed. "There was a bunch of them attacking one another, right in the middle of fighting. It was like they were just wanting to fight; it didn't matter who."

"They became the bitter imps of all the legends. The Brownies fought them in the shadows for a long time, trying to keep them from revealing all to the humans. Eventually, they were so reduced in number, they were considered no longer a threat. Only..."

"There were an awful lot of them yesterday." Blackie interrupted.

"Just so." Deirdre sounded a lot like Hypatia, Linn noted, smothering her smile in a bite of pasty. "We think... well, Dugan and I were talking a lot about this after, and before then Bronwyn, while we were hiding."

She made herself smaller, and Spot padded over silently and rested his big head on the cushion next to her. Dee petted him and he rumbled into a deep purr.

"It's ok, Dee." Blackie came and patted her arm awkwardly. "We're going to do something about it. But go on."

"I'm ok. It was just... well, what we talked about was how many there were. We think they must have been hiding, and breeding up their population to hold a war. I found a clue, in the book..."

"Where did you all come from? I mean the coblyns, and the gods." Linn asked. "Your uncle, I think, gave me some clues, and Coyote gave me some, and I pieced it together, but not all of it."

Dee sighed. "I'm not supposed to talk about it. The clue, in the book..."

"Dee, I'm going off on a very important mission in a day." Linn pointed out. "I think I need as much information as I can get."

"Let me tell you about this, and maybe that will be enough." Deirdre sat up straight. "There was a brownie squad who managed to listen to a goblin plan. Dugan wouldn't tell me what happened, but only two made it back here. What they said didn't make much sense, until I was reading the book.

"In the book, about a millennia ago, the clan head who broke off the goblins, or those who would become goblins, left a long letter, proclaiming that our race had suffered at the hands of the gods long enough, and it was time for us to reclaim our own power, and return to our true home. He wrote that Lir, the most ancient of ancients, had in his secret place the key to returning to the lost home."

"And Mac'Lir is Lir's son." Linn remembered that much of the Celtic myth class they had been taught.

Merrick shook his head. "No, Lir is Lir. Has always been, just with different names."

"That happened a lot." Linn thought of all the myths they had been taught. The ever-living, as Granny had called them, changed names and locales from time to time for concealment, or in the case of the Olympians, in an effort to keep power.

"Well, that explains why the goblins attacked as soon as they heard Mac'Lir was awake. They think he can get them back to their home." Blackie mused.

"And their lost glory days. According to the goblins, they were in charge, in this legendary place, and the titans and their children were the servants." Deirdre filled in. She fluttered her free hand. The other had a glass of iced tea in it. Dee seemed to like that a lot more than Linn had. "Now, I know that's not true. But whatever we once were, my people are now partners with those who were in charge then. Likely they were slaves, but we are as free as we want to be, unlike the goblins, who are enslaved by their own hatred and delusions."

"So that is what I have to do. I have to beat the goblins to Mac'Lir's secret place, which may hold the key to this lost universe where the gods and goblins came from, and protect it from them." Linn slumped back against the wall.

A deep voice answered her. "Not exactly. And not alone."

They all jumped to their feet as Mac'Lir walked into the room.

"M'- m'Lord!" Merrick stammered.

"Sit, sit. Boy, you must learn to treat me more like she does." Mac'Lir gestured at Linn. "The age of kings has passed, and I was never that happy to be one, anyway."

The young people all sat, and Mac'Lir stood, clasping his hands behind his back and looking down at the open book on the table. "What I need from you, Daughter of Fire, is the new knowledge, mingled with the old magic."

"It's not magic, sir." Linn protested.

"Oh, I know that now. I am... I would have said I was learning, a thousand years all at once, but I came to find that I am remembering. And what is magic? That word will do well enough."

"Someone once told me that technology, sufficiently advanced, became indistinguishable from magic." Linn shot back at him.

"Ah! My dear girl, this is why you are perfect for the task."

Linn subsided. Mac'Lir had an air about him. She just didn't want to argue with him, or not much, anyway. He smiled down at her. "I'm old fashioned, girl. Bear with me."

He really was a charming old fellow. Linn smiled back.

"I am remembering." Mac'Lir turned back to the book. "I suppose that is what I have been trying to do, when I accumulated all these records, and left standing orders to keep adding to the library. Which seems to have grown like a weed patch." He wandered into the shelves, still talking. "I know what they say, that I am the oldest of the ancients. But it isn't true."

He reappeared, a cobweb on his fingers where he had wiped it out of his hair. He was shaking his hand to dislodge it. "I am not the oldest. But I have lived so long, I have outlived my own memories. What is left is as cobwebby and dusty as this collection of knowledge. Which is why I need you, Daughter of Fire."

"To do what?" She asked. Maybe this time he would answer.

13

REAL MISSION

"*I* need you to answer questions we have forgotten how to ask." Mac'Lir carefully turned a page in the book. "This, I can grasp, answer, and fight against. But what secrets lie elsewhere, I cannot. You, perhaps, can. Magic; as you say, technology."

That word sounded odd coming from him, as he didn't pronounce it quite correctly.

"So, I am going to be looking at technology," she asked, wanting clarity, "when I get where you send me... us?"

All of them were paying attention now. Mac'Lir looked around the room, at five sets of bright eyes. "I am not sending all of you, fear not, little daughter."

He was addressing Deirdre, who nodded a little. Then he spoke to Linn again.

"Yes, but you may not recognize it. You must strain your imagination, I expect." Mac'Lir walked toward the door. "You will leave tomorrow afternoon. I am not sending you until your mother gives me leave, but I cannot wait much longer."

"I'm ready." Linn told him.

He paused in the doorway, looking down at her. "I know you are, brave girl."

He was gone before Linn could respond. "I'm no hero."

Deirdre snorted from her chair. "Yes, you are."

"What? All I did was charge headlong into a fight. I'm not even supposed to be in a battle, the grown-ups have worked hard enough to protect all of us kids." Linn stood up and winced as her leg pulled on the regrowing muscle.

"You were spectacularly heroic in battle." Dee pointed out, laughing. "Dancing on a troll?"

"I wasn't dancing! Merrick..." Linn turned to him.

"Unh-uh. I was under the darned thing." He raised his injured hand, fending her off. "Hey, ow!"

Linn had batted him on the back of the head. "Why didn't you tell me that before? I didn't mean to drop a troll on you."

"Linn, you didn't mean to, but it was the only thing you could have done." Blackie broke in. "Well, okay, you could have run away like a smart person..."

Merrick laughed. "I'm not mad at you, Linn. If you hadn't dropped it on me, it would have smashed me flatter."

Linn shivered. "I'm trying really hard not to think too much about the whole scene. I could have lost any of you. And I kept looking down... for Dee."

Linn walked over to her friend and knelt by the chair. "I was so afraid I'd find you, or Spot, out there."

"I was sensibly hiding in the wine cellar, with all who could not sally forth. I know my limitations." Dee's lip wobbled, betraying her calm tone.

"You're the smart one of us." Linn reassured her. "It was a stinky, beastly, painful experience."

"Yeah." Merrick unfolded himself from the chair. "You're lucky you were out of it. Look, Dee, you're the brain. I haven't known you long, but you have more smarts than... well, okay, maybe not more than Linn. But different."

"Which means you're the brawn?" Deirdre giggled. "You are smart too. C'mon, Blackie, what are you?"

"Oh, I'm lazy." The tall boy sprawled out in his chair. "I was running for the gate. Stopped to fend off the nasty little monsters along my way."

"You're a terrible liar, Blackie." Deirdre rapped her knuckles on Linn's head.

"Ow, what was that for?" Linn rubbed her skull.

"Stop sitting at my feet. I'm not an invalid or your mother." Deirdre pointed at the table. "But you can get me a pasty, now you're up."

Linn obligingly handed her one from the section Bronwyn had said were sweets, and got one for herself. "Well, who wants to come with me?"

She looked at them, they had all stopped chewing or talking and were staring at her. "What? I'm the one being sent, it's my job. I'm not going to assume you're trailing along, unless you want it. It might be dangerous. Dee, you're staying here, and I need you to keep digging..." Linn pointed with the hand that held her pastry, scattering crumbs. Deirdre squeaked indignantly. "Sorry. Yeah, anyway... I'm only taking volunteers."

Merrick snorted. "You're dreadful at recruitment."

"Wasn't trying to recruit." Linn pointed out, sitting back on her stones.

"You know I'm coming." Blackie said quietly.

Linn nodded. One day she was going to have a long talk with him about following her everywhere, and what was up with that? But it would wait. She would have missed him badly.

"And me." Merrick stretched. "But after a good night's sleep."

Spot nodded at Linn, and rested his chin on Dee's arm again, almost knocking her off the chair as she had been getting up. "You big buffoon," the little coblyn girl rubbed his ears. "We need to clean up," she informed the group tartly.

"Sorry about the crumbs." Linn shoved the last bite in her mouth, and started piling the glasses and pitcher onto the nearly empty platter. Dee produced a little whisk broom, and Blackie was handed a rag to wipe off the table. Merrick hoisted the book.

"Oof! Dee, how do you manage this thing? It's made of lead..."

She took it from him. "No, just leather over wood panels, and various papers and vellums."

"You're stronger than you look." He released the book to her and picked up the platter. "See you all in the morning."

Linn found herself back in her room shortly, and sat on the bed. She felt like someone had opened a tap and let all her energy run out. Finally alone, she touched her face gingerly. If anything, the places where the acid had burned felt smoother than the old skin. It was sore if she pressed, but didn't hurt otherwise. Unlike her leg, which was aching, a mass of charley horses marching up and down with nails in their shoes. Linn flopped backward on the bed with a whimper.

There was a quiet knock at the door.

"Who is it?" Linn asked, still staring at the ceiling.

"Your mother."

"C'mon in Mom." Linn was still trying to sit up when Theta closed the door behind herself.

"Stay put." Linn felt her mother pick up the uninjured leg and pull her shoe off. Then she unlaced the other one and wiggled it gently off.

Linn gritted her teeth.

"That bad, huh?" Theta asked. "Can you get up enough to get out of clothes? Then I will do more healing on you."

"Oh, I'm ok..." Linn rolled to her side and levered herself up. She felt like she was made of jello. "I was fine until I got in here, anyway."

"Your body needs to rest." Theta said firmly, helping Linn undress. "You slept for three days, yes, but it still needs more time."

"I'm leaving tomorrow." Linn rolled under the covers. "I have to be better then."

"I know you are." Theta leaned over her and brushed loose hair off her face. "I'm proud of you, kiddo. But listen to your body, and don't push too hard. If you collapse, what happens to your quest?"

"Yeah." Linn closed her eyes. "I'll be goo..."

If she dreamed, she never remembered it afterward.

When she woke up in the morning, she popped up out of the bed. She had remembered something important. Well, important to her, anyway.

Linn scrambled back into her modern clothes, and went looking for her mother. She found her having breakfast in the kitchen with Bronwyn.

"Mom!" Linn bent over and gave her a sideways hug. "Where is Bes?"

"Wondered when you would ask that. Sit, eat."

Linn sat, and Bronwyn pushed a plate at her.

Theta propped her chin on her hands. "Bes is... incognito right now.

He left a note for you. And you know, Linn, he wouldn't have left you alone unless it were absolutely necessary."

Linn nodded and took the folded piece of paper. She opened it and laughed. "He's written it in hieroglyphics."

Linn showed it to Bronwyn. "Oh, my... how colorful. Can you read that?"

"No, not really. But I can puzzle it out, and I know it means he's in good humor." Linn put it in her pocket for later. "Bronwyn, what do you put in your eggs?"

The brownie lady chuckled, pleased. "A pinch of thyme, my dear. Does my heart good to see you young people enjoy your food."

"You're a really good cook." Linn assured her, cleaning her plate.

Linn went to the library after she'd had her breakfast, sure she would find Dee there. The room looked empty when she walked in, but there was a faint rustling behind the shelves.

"Dee?" Linn walked into the maze of shelves, then around another corner. "Good grief, I had no idea it was this large."

Linn stared down a narrow passageway that led off between innumerable shelves on either side. The same chaos that you could see in the first room prevailed here, too. "Dee? I'm not coming in there after you, I'll get lost!"

"Keep your pants on," came faintly from the stacks.

"I'm hardly undressing in the library." Linn put her hands on her hips. "Did you sleep last night?" she demanded as her friend walked toward her, cobwebs lying across her hair like a veil.

"Yes." Deirdre was carrying an armful of vellum scrolls.

"Stop..." Linn pulled the upper edge of the web, white with dust. "I swear, you're married to your job. Look at this!" She held up the tattered web.

Dee dissolved in giggles. "I really need to clean, don't I?"

"This isn't really your library," Linn pointed out.

Dee piled the scrolls on the empty table. "Well, actually..."

"Wait a minute. Have you eaten?" Linn interrupted, suspicious.

"Not yet. But-"

"I knew it! C'mon." Linn tried to pull Dee toward the door, but the coblyn dug in her heels.

"If you'd listen to me! Merrick is bringing a tray. And yes, this is my library. Mac'Lir offered me the librarian position."

Linn let go of her friend's arm and felt her own mouth drop open. "Dee!"

Deirdre laughed. "Hypatia is coming to give me some help in a week. Pretty neat, huh?"

Merrick walked in with the tray of food. "Hey, Linn. Dee, where do you want this?"

"Did she tell you she's the official librarian now?" Linn turned on him.

He nodded. "The last one died of sheer old age when I was about three. Hopefully Dee will get some interesting books in, now..."

"So that's why you're buttering me up?" Dee was back in her chair with a plate, eating.

"Maybe." The boy gave them both a wolfish grin. "That, and mission intel. You could save our hides."

Linn grinned back at him. "That's why I'm here."

She was feeling excited about it, today. Going off to save the world? A whole lot better than wasting away surfing and in school. They weren't going to have to fight goblins again, just figure out ancient technology, and the prospect of that had her positively drooling. Up until now, everything was based on hints she had worked out, from Coyote, Deirdre's uncle, and other things. That, and a stubborn refusal to accept 'it's magic' as an answer for anything.

"I don't know what I have for you." Dee poured tea, hot this time.

"Nothing?" Merrick took the cup she handed him. "Thanks."

"Not nothing. I worry that it's worse than nothing, though."

"Dee, stop twitching, and let's see if the group makes sense of it. Where are Blackie and Spot?" Linn sat back on her personal pile of stones.

"Still asleep, last I saw." Merrick offered. "Big pile of fur on the bed."

Linn chuckled. They did rather resemble oversized housecats at times. "Merrick, you grew up here too, right? With Dee?"

He shook his head. "My mam took me to Earth, to Ballentrae, when I was four. She worried about me, here." Merrick looked into his teacup as though seeing something for a moment. "She didn't think the wolf-shifting was natural."

That explained a lot. "I'm sorry." she offered.

He shrugged. "I had the stories, and then last year, Dad brought me here again. It's- I loved Mam, but..."

He drank his tea. Linn leaned forward. "Is your mother...?"

"No, no... just still on Earth. It was time for me to grow up, but she didn't want to let go."

"Um." Linn wasn't sure what to say, now. Here her mother was, patching her up and sending her back off to the wars.

"Eh." Merrick tossed back his tea. "Dee, break it to us gentle."

"Well, I went looking for clues based on what Mac'Lir said about technology. I know the gods are all under a geas not to talk about where they came from, except in the vaguest of terms."

Linn nodded. She'd found that out from Bes and her grandfather shortly after learning part of the secrets of her own ancestry.

"Hang on. Why can there be a geas if there isn't really magic?" Merrick asked. "I mean, all my life I've known I was under one, so? How is it possible?"

"Programming, I think." Linn set her cup back on the tray. She was beginning to really look forward to home, soda, and coffee. "If as I suspect what we know of as magic are really clouds of microscopic robots, processing on the quantum movements at an atomic level..."

Blackie walked in. "Then that explains me," he added without missing a beat. "Did you guys eat it all without me?"

"Well, it certainly explains why you can eat so much and not be fat as a tick." Linn watched him pile a plate.

"Gotta fuel the magic." He answered around a mouthful of food, settling into a chair.

Linn rolled her eyes. She almost preferred him silent and four-pawed. "Where was I?"

"Explaining how robots control our brains." Deirdre added helpfully.

"It's not control, it's conditioning. For some reason, the first people who came to earth didn't want to talk about where they came from, or why. But what I can't figure out is why all of them seem to have agreed to the limitations."

"Maybe they didn't." Merrick shrugged when they all looked at him, "I don't think I would have."

"Which means something forced them. Like your family was forced into protecting Mac'Lir's children all those years ago."

He squirmed a little. "You do know I'm still under that geas, right?"

"What, you don't want to protect children?" Blackie asked with a smirk.

Merrick glared at him. "Yes, but only if I get a choice in the matter!"

Linn stepped in between them. "We're completely off topic. Dee never got to say what she learned."

The boys subsided. Linn didn't think they were really angry with one another, but this silly sparring was going to have to stop. They had been picking on one another since they had first met.

"I think you're going to Iceland. Land of ice and fire, and all that. I also think I know why Mac'Lir awakened now." Dee unrolled a vellum scroll.

Linn bent over it. Deirdre pointed at a little fleck on the map. "The bit here... it's a volcanic island off the coast of Iceland."

"How old is this map?" Linn asked.

"I'm not sure... no date on it. Or not that I can see. There's squiggles."

Linn could see them around the edge. "So, what does this have to do...?"

"This same island reappeared just a few years ago." Dee unrolled a very modern map on top of the old one. Linn could see the familiar logo in bright yellow letters.

"You think that is where Mac'Lir was?"

"It would explain why he'd vanished entirely for so long. For a while, after legends say he went over the sea, he'd come back when called. Then, even that stopped."

Linn looked at her. Dee had paused dramatically. "What?"

"Because the island had sunk beneath the sea again."

"Wait, we're going to an island that could sink again at any minute?"

Merrick got up and looked at the map. "One good thing, I doubt the goblins can get there on their own."

"But we'd better hurry." Linn sighed. "Speaking of which, what time is it?"

14

SWAN SKIN

$\mathcal{M}$ ac'Lir was in his Great Hall, leaning on one elbow in his throne. He didn't look like he had slept, or breakfasted, either.

"Daughter of Fire." His voice was deep and tired.

Linn stepped up onto the dais again. She wondered why there was never anyone but her up on this thing, close to him. "Mac'Lir."

He smiled up at her. "You are too big to ask you to sit on the arm of my chair, child. And yet... not old enough to send you out on this errand. But I have no choice. There simply isn't time, or enough of us..."

"It's okay, sir." Linn wasn't sure why she was reassuring him, but then he got that twinkle back in his eye.

"You're not afraid of me, are you?"

Linn shook her head, wondering what he was getting at.

"Good." Mac'Lir reached down next to his chair and picked something up. When Linn could see it, she realized what it was. The swan bag.

He put it in his lap and stroked the white feathers. "All I have left of her."

"I know the story." Linn said quietly.

"Oh, do you?" He looked at her, his stormy eyes bright.

"Granny Clinch told us." Linn looked at the bag. "I'm sorry for your loss."

"She's still with me, while I have this. And..." He closed his eyes. "You have the sight?"

Linn closed her eyes. She could see a blue and green light from the bag. It was deeply imbued with power, from two sources. One was him, the other must have been Aoife. She opened her eyes.

"I see what you mean." She felt very serious all at once.

"The wonderful thing about her gift to me, is that when you reach into this bag, you pull out what you really need. Almost magic, isn't it?" Mac'Lir winked at her.

Linn suspected her mother had been telling tales. "Almost," she agreed.

"Are you ready to go?" He opened the mouth of the bag.

"I think so. We're wanting to get it over with."

"Reach in. You'll find what you need."

He lifted the sack so it hung free, reaching down to the floor in front of him, the white feathers shimmering. Linn took a deep breath and reached down, into the empty folds. She didn't believe in magic, it was silly.

The bag hit the floor with a thud, and she touched a nylon handle. Linn wrapped her fingers around it and lifted, and Mac'Lir held the bag open with both hands now, and her bundle was good-sized. Linn watched as Mac'Lir stroked the feathers again before he tucked the bag away.

"What have you got?" He leaned forward.

Linn was holding a black case, rectangular, black nylon over steel, it felt like. She set it down and popped the clips, then knelt to open the case. Inside the top of the case were pockets, zippered, with first aid supplies in them. In the bottom of the case, in shock-resistant foam, was an odd-looking laptop.

"What is that?" Mac'Lir asked as Linn pressed the power button.

"It's a computer." Linn told him. "I'm not sure what some of these cables are for."

She held up a handful of neatly bundled cords. On one end, they were ordinary USB tips, the other ends weren't familiar at all. The computer chimed.

"Well, this isn't right." She frowned at the screen. A blinking cursor was the only thing showing.

"All I know is that it will be what you need." The king settled back. "I must ask if you can leave as soon as possible. I have heard back from my men in the field, and they say the goblin army is on the move. But they don't know yet where the goblins are going."

"And you're afraid they are headed to where your, er, secrets are?" Linn shut the computer back down by pressing the power button until the cursor went away and she could feel through her fingertips that the hard drive had stilled. She zipped the case back up and stood. The first aid supplies had her worried. She'd been trained, they all had, in the basics. But if the swan bag gave what was needed, it implied they were important.

"Yes. Please hurry, Daughter of Fire. You will understand when you reach your destination."

He held out his hand, and she solemnly took it. Then she walked out of the room, Blackie and Merrick falling in behind her. She was headed for the gate, and then they would take the High Path. Mac'Lir's touch on her hand had reactivated the feather marking he'd given her, and Linn could feel the warmth of the power as it keyed to where they were going.

At the gate, she faltered, looking out over what was left of the garden. There were no bodies... she wondered for a fleeting moment how on earth they had moved the massive troll. But the flowers and herbs she'd seen that first day were mostly gone. Bare patches of earth mystified her, until it dawned on her that it must have been troll blood, or maybe just clean-up of remains. Linn swallowed hard, and dragged her mind back to what they were doing now. Which shouldn't involve goblins, and swords, and blood. Linn wondered what had happened to Lambent, but now was not the time.

"Ready? Stow your gear." She had showed them how to do the trick with the in-between places her grandmother had taught her. Linn had her backpack there, and now the computer case. She really hoped she didn't need a change of clothes; she didn't have one with her any longer.

Then she stepped calmly forward, and into the High Path, the boys on her heels. Linn could feel her stomach tighten, and the feather on her palm tugging. This time, she knew they had to hurry, and had a lot more on the line.

The boys behind her were silent. She knew they were nervous, too, even if they wouldn't admit it. She really hated never knowing what they would find at the end of the path. As it turned out, it wasn't much. The tiny island wasn't wet all over, but you could see all of it from where they stood on the lip of the shallow caldera. A tiny trickle of steam rose from the center of it, and Linn decided that they had better avoid that. Every time she moved, a slide of the loose pumice cascaded into the caldera, making her nervous. She was more used to the solid lava flows of the Hawaiian Islands, although she'd seen this in a few places. It wasn't a good place to be walking around.

"I have no idea what we are looking for." The wind took her words away, but Merrick nodded. They were both wearing heavy coats now, having pulled them from storage on their arrival, and realization that it was bitterly cold. Blackie, in cat form, had puffed his fur out until he was half-again as large as he had been, and gone prowling. Linn and Merrick had made their way around the rim of the caldera without seeing anything more than clouds of seabirds.

"Use your other sight." Merrick shouted. "I don't know about you, but I'd like some shelter. He can't have been out in the open on this nub of land for centuries."

Linn nodded mutely. It was a good suggestion. She held out her hands. "I don't want to fall!"

With Merrick's warm hands grasping her wrists, and hers on his sturdy forearms, she closed her eyes and looked for power with her own.

"Darn. Nothing. We'll have to move again." Linn's eyes snapped open, and she looked at Blackie, who was prowling with his nose to the ground, for all the world like a dog.

Merrick followed her gaze. "I could do that."

"You could, if you want to sniff seaweed and bird droppings." Linn chuckled at the look on his face. "Or you can make sure I don't blow off this rock while my eyes are closed. Let's move over there."

She pointed. He didn't let go of her hand while they moved to the other side of the caldera, a process which took some time. Linn decided she didn't mind. It kept her hand warmer, and it turned out two people were better balanced working together than separate. He stopped and held out his free hand, and she took it. Then he took a step closer to her, startling her.

Merrick tucked both their hands into his parka pockets. "C'mon then, have a look!" He didn't have to shout; they were so close now. Linn closed her eyes. He was also shielding her partly from the wind, which felt good. She focused on her power, trying to remember where she had scanned from before, and started there.

Linn had hoped she would know it when she saw it, and she did. She pulled one hand away from Merrick and pointed. "There!"

Then she opened her eyes. The glowing white aura she had seen vanished, but she had a pretty good idea of where it was. Blackie came loping to meet them as they scrambled down the side of the hill. When they were halfway, Linn stopped her descent by the simple expedient of dropping herself into a sit, and using her butt as an anchor. Merrick crouched beside her as she focused again.

"It's right there." Linn reached out, and picked up a handful of rocks. "But I don't know how to reach it."

"Maybe it's not on earth?" Merrick offered. Blackie was staring intently at the patch of ground with his eyes narrowed.

Linn shook her head. "I wouldn't see it if it weren't here."

Blackie stepped forward slowly, looking as though he were stalking prey, and vanished, an inch at a time, into midair.

"I think he's got it!" Merrick grabbed the tip of the big cat's tail gently, and followed him in. He stuck a hand back out, and Linn grabbed onto it and let him tow her through a tingling field of power.

"Whew!" She ran her hands through her hair, with the wind and the static discharge, it was puffed out like a dandelion head. Linn looked around. They were in a crudely hewn tunnel, which had been painted bright white at some point, and lights in the ceiling flickered to life as they moved. Motion detectors. She didn't see wiring, though.

Merrick cleared his throat. "Would you, ah..."

Linn looked at him, wondering what he was suddenly all shy about. "What?"

"It's just, if you could go that way..." he pointed deeper into the tunnel, "but not too far? And turn your back."

"Oh. Sure." Linn started to walk away, following Blackie, who was moving at a slow amble, looking in every direction and sniffing the floors from time to time. She heard the ticking of toenails coming up behind her, and felt the furry skull slip under her fingertips just before he bumped her hip with his shoulder.

"Feel more prepared, now?"

The big gray wolf nodded, and paced up to Blackie, who reached out a paw and pushed at his head, roughly. Merrick swung his body sideways and thumped the big cat against the near wall. Formalities out of the way, the boys proceeded in formation ahead of Linn. She glanced over her shoulder. There was no way to get in aside from the way they had, and the island was deserted. Still, you always wanted to keep an eye on what was behind you.

They moved slowly, with both the boys using noses as much as eyes. Merrick looked back and her and nodded his head deliberately. Mac'Lir had been here, that meant.

Linn nodded back. The corridor tunnel was sloping downward now, and she felt like it had a familiar construction. The lava tunnels at Sanctuary were like this. The bit at the top had looked hand-dug, though. She wondered about that. Were they still on earth, or the high plane where the gods dwelled? Was the high plane a replica of Earth? Not exactly, she didn't think, but then again where Mac'Lir's castle was looked a lot like a wilder Scotland. And Quetzalcoatl's Court was very like the Yucatan Peninsula looked on google. She had been to the Mayan god's court, but not to the equivalent on Earth in real life.

If they were still on Earth, in Iceland, then there was a lot of power involved in keeping this place safe from the active tectonic plates.

"Hold on a minute." Linn told the boys, then stopped and closed her eyes. It was like looking at the sun through closed eyelids. White, with tinges of other colors, a lot or reds and yellows. She didn't think she'd met the yellow power before, but likely it was one of the Olympians, and she was just as glad to not have that dubious pleasure. She was overwhelmed and dazzled by the display, and had to blink to adjust when she opened her eyes again. The tunnel looked dim after the sight she had just seen.

"It's like nothing I've ever seen." Linn told the boys. "There's a huge amount of power, and either it's from many sources, or not from our ancestors at all. Let's keep going, but slow."

She didn't think there would be booby traps, or Mac'Lir would have warned them. But she wanted time to think and assess as they started downward again. It was steeper, now. She could see the slope, and the tunnel was coiling round on itself. Merrick and Blackie fell back so she wouldn't lose sight of them around a corner, and slowly, they kept moving toward the bowels of the Earth.

15

FROST

*L*inn stopped them after a while and checked the time. They had been walking for an hour.

"Break, liquids, and let's talk a bit?" Linn was already pulling her backpack out to get water. She turned her head politely to let the boys come back to human for and get their own gear.

"How far are we going to walk?" Blackie asked, leaning against the wall, his legs stretched out in front of him. She knew he wasn't tired already, just bored. Featureless tunnel was, well, boring.

"Until we get there." Linn stopped. "That was my mom coming out my mouth just now, wasn't it?"

"You're officially the adult." Merrick agreed.

"Joy." Linn got up. "I sit any longer I'm going to get stiff." She stuffed her pack back out of sight, and started down the tunnel.

She'd gone around a curve, and when she heard paws behind her, she held up one hand to stop them. "Shh... listen."

She could hear a humming: faint, and it more came through her feet than was heard. Merrick bumped her with his head. "Okay, so you hear it too. I think we're close."

The humming got progressively annoying, like off-kilter speakers, as they got closer. Blackie would stop and shake his head from time to time, but Merrick got to the point where he had to stop and whimper.

"Change, Merrick. It's not so bad to human ears. Or can you hear like a wolf in human form?"

He shifted. Linn was startled, he was usually so careful to do that privately. She didn't see anything, really, it was a blur of skin, fur, and glowing power, just like Sekhmet. Linn made a mental note to introduce the two of them. Then he was kneeling on the tunnel floor, fully dressed, and holding his heads in his hands.

Linn got Tylenol for him, and a bottle of water. He gave her a grateful look out of reddened eyes.

"Do you want to retreat back up the tunnel?" Linn tried to offer him a way out. He shook his head and got up. She took that as a no.

"Onward." Linn stepped out in front this time.

The curves had been getting tighter, and now she came around a corner and into a vast room. Linn stopped and stared. Above, the ceiling was not terribly high, perhaps only twelve feet. But the far side of the room was shrouded in mist, and the walls to each side of her curved slightly. The room was oblong, from what she could see.

Scattered across it were low pillars. She headed toward the nearest one, zipping up her coat. The room was cold, too. Frost glittered on the pillar, which wasn't so low, when she got to it. The top came to her chest. It was rectangular, and vaguely coffin-shaped. Linn had forgotten the hum, but Merrick grabbed her.

"Can we find where the hum is coming from and shut it up?" He was still rubbing his temple.

"Yeah, let's start there. Can you tell a direction?"

He nodded. "Blackie can help, even more."

The big cat stropped against Merrick's leg.

"Gerroff me, you big lug." Merrick cuffed Blackie's head, but Linn noted that it was gentle.

Blackie headed toward the far side of the room, with Merrick and Linn following. None of them wanted to get closer, and Linn wasn't sure she could do anything with the noise, but it wouldn't hurt to look. Maybe it would be an easy fix.

The mist, which Linn was sure was due to the cold in the room, got thicker as they got near the wall. It was harder to see here, because of it, and Linn stumbled over a pillar. This one wasn't even knee high.

"Ouch." She stopped to rub her shin, and Blackie re-emerged from the fog to head-bump her, his ears tickling her chin. "I'm coming. I wonder why these ones are so much shorter."

She was also worried about the fog. How were they supposed to find something in this mess?

When she bumped into the console, she was no longer as worried about the fog. Now, Linn was worried about figuring out what they had here, and how big it was. Machinery stretched off to either side of them. Lights glowed on some of it, other parts looked like they ought to be lit up but were dark.

The humming had gotten loud enough to be an annoying whine, with intermittent rumbles that she could feel through her feet. Something wasn't right, she knew that in her bones. It was very unsettling. Linn stared at the strange panel in front of her, suddenly and utterly convinced that technology was indeed magic. She could no more fix anything here than a cave man could.

"Dang it." She kicked at the machine.

Blackie nudged her, and pointed with his ears off to her left. Linn sighed. It wouldn't help, but she might as well look.

Merrick was sitting on one of the low pillars. "Come on." Linn held her hand out. "I don't want to lose you in this maze."

He nodded without speaking. His skin was pale and sweaty looking, despite the chilly air. Linn was worried about him. He clung to her hand as they followed Blackie through the tendrils of mist. She needed to either make the noise stop, or get him out of here. He was stubborn enough that she didn't think the second thing was an option.

The noise was louder, know, and she found Blackie sitting and looking up at a door. He could manage doors with lever or pressure handles, not a round doorknob, or as this one had, a keypad. Linn looked at it closely. The symbols were strange, almost runic, nothing she could recognize as numbers, but it still made her think of a numerical keypad. It was slightly raised from the door's surface, and in one side was a small hole, strangely shaped.

"Oh..." Linn stepped back, and transferred Merrick's hand to the scruff of Blackie's neck. "Look, I know you two aren't close, but I need both my hands. Since you..." she looked at Blackie. "Don't want to be human right now, and Merrick is..." she looked at him. His eyes were glassy, and he didn't seem to be processing what she was saying.

"Okay, I'm going to hurry now."

When she'd seen the tiny hole, Linn had known they were on the right track. Now, hands-free, she pulled free the case Aoife's skin had given her. It wasn't magic, she told herself firmly. It was analysis of all the possible outcomes, and then the vector indicated which pivotal point it all hung on. Hence, the case. She'd recognized the shape of the reset hole on the side of the keypad.

Linn booted the computer up, and connected the right cable from it to the keypad. For a moment, nothing happened, and she was afraid she had guessed wrong. Then the screen filled with the mysterious symbols, and the keypad beeped. She could hear the click as the door unlocked.

Before she went through the door, she used a bit of the medical tape to keep the door from being able to relock, and put the computer away. She might need it again.

Linn looked at the boys. Merrick was sitting on the floor now, his eyes closed, and one arm around Blackie's neck. She knelt next to him.

"I think we need to go back."

"Mmm-mm." He shook his head.

"Look, I know you're a guy, and stubborn, and all." Linn started.

He spoke without opening his eyes. "I can't."

"What's wrong?" Linn reached out and felt his pulse. It was racing, but strong. His skin felt clammy.

"I can't see, the light's blinding me, and there are colors around stuff." He gritted out. "And I'm gonna throw up."

"Okay, something is definitely wrong with you." Linn rocked back on her heels. "I'm going to get you out of here."

"No. Get the noise. It's important." Merrick batted her hand away.

Linn sighed and got up. "I'll hurry."

She turned away, muttering "Men" under her breath.

The room through the door was clear of the mist, and much smaller and warmer. Linn stood and looked before she started moving. It looked like a space station or something from a movie. Everything was white, and rounded, and... Her shoulders sagged. How on earth was this going to work? She closed her eyes and opened the sight.

Then she opened them again, and rubbed her eyes, blinking tears away. That had hurt. If power was nanobots, this room was full of them. Maybe even a source of them. Linn looked down at her hand, where the feather was. It was glowing brightly. It didn't hurt, but she felt funny.

"Okay," Linn said out loud to herself. "I need to get out of here quickly."

She took a deep breath, and then regretted it. It felt like she had sucked in something sharp. Coughing, she started to walk around the room and look for the noise.

Linn didn't find it. But she did find a part of the walls that wasn't glowing. Elsewhere, the walls were lit, and on smooth patches, the symbols flickered over them. Here, it was just dark. She sighed, and started looking closer, for an access panel, or something.

She found, near the floor, another raised keypad like the one on the door. It was knee-high to her, and she sat on the floor in confusion. Why was it so short? At least she had stopped coughing. Her head felt clear, even a little giddy. She really needed to get out of here.

The reset hole was the same as the one on the door. She plugged the computer in. After a moment, the screen filled up with symbols. This time, however, there was no beep. Instead, two boxes appeared at the bottom of the screen. Linn stared at the cursor blinking in one of them. Password? Code? Who knew?

The keyboard was in English. She stared at it for a while, but it didn't yield any answers, either. Linn closed her eyes, and poked at the keyboard. A few clicks later, she opened her eyes again and wiped away the tears. She looked up at the wall, which was flickering back to life. There was a series of large clicks, and then a whoosh of noise.

Linn hit the floor. It was roaring past her, she realized after a second. Behind the wall. She got up slowly, looking around cautiously. The whining seemed to have stopped. Blackie opened the door and looked in.

"You shifted." Linn said stupidly.

"Get out of there! Linn..." He beckoned at her. "C'mon!"

Linn staggered to her feet, and then bent back down to scoop up the computer. She didn't bother to power it down. Clutching it to her chest, she wove toward the door. It was impossible, she found, to walk in a straight line with her head swimming the way it was.

Blackie seemed oddly reluctant to come into the room, he was just standing there holding both his arms out to her, the door propped on one foot. Linn reached him and pushed the computer at him. He took it reflexively, and as she pushed past him; he took his foot out of the door and it closed behind them.

Linn saw Merrick still sitting on the floor and pointed herself at him. He was looking up at her, with his eyes open, and clear.

"Oh... goo'you shee me." Linn could hear herself, and she sounded weird. "Um."

The room went into a small spin, and she lost her footing. Merrick caught her on the way down. "Oh, I feel funny." Linn heard herself say in a very small voice. Then she closed her eyes because the room was making her seasick. "No light."

She wasn't sure later if she had said that out loud. She did know that she must have passed out, because she woke up wrapped in space blankets, cuddled up to Merrick, who was sound asleep. Experimentally, Linn closed her eyes. There was a faint glow around the nearby equipment, and some far-away bright flares, but the blinding power of the small room was out of her sight. She sighed.

Merrick and the blankets were warm, and Linn wasn't looking forward to the chill of the vast room. But it was awkward to be cuddling with her friend. She squirmed away, tucking the blankets around him as she moved, trying not to wake him up. He rolled over and sighed, and she froze. But his eyes were still closed, and he didn't move again. Linn finished making her escape.

Blackie, back in cat form, was curled up on his other side. He opened one golden eye, and then yawned widely, displaying white fangs. Linn glared at him. Her head ached.

"I need answers, buster. Get over here where we can talk." She hissed across the sleeping Merrick.

Linn looked around the room. It looked much brighter in here... then she realized that the fog had receded. She remembered the whooshing of the previous night, or however long it had been, and decided that what she had reactivated had been connected to the ventilation in this room somehow.

Quietly, she walked away from the sleeping Merrick and waited for Blackie.

He tapped her on the shoulder, in human form. Linn spun around and tried to keep her voice down.

"What did you know, and when did you know it?"

He leaned back a little. "Whoa, there."

"I have the headache from Hades, there is no coffee, and..." She sighed. "I'm sorry, I shouldn't snap at you."

"I couldn't tell you, I needed to stay cat."

"What? And why?" Linn sat on the short column. She rubbed her temples.

Blackie sat next to her. "I can see things, as a cat, I can't as a human. Like the power in something, or..." He waved a hand to indicate the whole room. "Someplace. It's how I saw the tunnel door first, and then was able to go through it by focusing on merging my power with it. Which passed on to your... er, nanobots, through Merrick. I don't know if he can see like I can, we haven't talked about it."

"And the room last night? And what was wrong with Merrick? I still don't even know if he's going to be okay."

Blackie patted her hand. "He'll be fine. He was having a migraine induced by that noise, his ears are really sensitive even in human form."

Linn nodded, reassured by this. She looked toward where Merrick was still sleeping. She'd let him rest as long as possible.

"What about me, then?"

"You have a hangover." Blackie grinned when she glared at him. "Sorry, but you should have seen yourself last night, staggering and slurring. You were drunker than a skunk."

"And just how..." Linn paused in thought.

"The power level in that room was off the charts. You were in there a long time, absorbing it. I think you got an overdose." He sobered, the silly grin dropping away. "I was afraid it would hurt you, or even kill you, if you didn't come out."

Linn rubbed her head again. It was really hurting now. "I didn't even realize it. Yeah, it felt funny, and I knew the power level was high, but..."

Blackie shrugged. "It was pretty subtle at first, yeah. But you were glowing after you came out." He squinted at her. "You still glow, a lot brighter than normal."

"I fixed the problem, I think. But I don't think I fixed Mac'Lir's problem." She told him.

"How come?"

Linn turned over her palm and showed him the feather. It was flaring with a white light, pulsing with every beat of her heart. "Something's happening, Blackie, and I don't know what."

16

EAT WHEN YOU CAN

*T*hey both stared at her mark for a moment. It was kinda pretty, Linn had to admit, but she would prefer it on someone else.

"Do you..." Blackie asked slowly, "feel a direction?"

"Not really," Linn shook her head. "But maybe if I stand up and move around?"

"I'll wake Merrick." Blackie got up.

"And I'll fix breakfast." Linn muttered. She pulled her pack out and spread a selection of water bottles, protein bars, and trail mix out on the flat column. Merrick looked a little bloodshot in the eyes.

"Sorry to wake you." Linn held out a water bottle to him.

"Ungh." He chugged the bottle and took a deep breath, then another. "Okay, I'm better." He sat on the other side of the column and took a protein bar. "I suppose a hot breakfast is out of the question."

"We're roughing it." Linn kept her face expressionless.

He looked around and chuckled. Blackie wolfed down his food.

"Why are you not in a hurry?" he asked Linn.

"Because practically the first thing Bes taught me was not to start on an empty stomach."

"And how did he teach you that?" Merrick chased his protein bar with another water bottle and a handful of trail mix.

"By sending me out with no breakfast until I could catch my own." Linn remembered that. It hadn't been as easy to get a rabbit as the books made it out to be. She had been very hungry by the time she had one, late that evening.

Blackie was positively bouncing. "Are you ready now?"

She looked around the area, and picked up a scrap of wrapper. "Now I am."

"Bes teach you to police your camp, too?"

"No, that was Grandpa Heff, when I was 7. He tanned my hide." Linn rubbed her backside in reminiscence.

"You are not a normal girl," Merrick proclaimed with a strong note of approval.

"Nope." Linn started to walk toward the other side of the room, paying attention to her hand.

The fog was clear on the end of the room where they had come in. Linn could see the low archway of the tunnel mouth from here. They were perhaps halfway down the room, although... she turned and looked downward. There was a slight slope, but she couldn't see how far it went.

"That way." She pointed into the mist.

The boys followed her. Linn walked slowly, unwilling to rush into the unknown. Look how much trouble it had almost gotten her in already. Her head still ached. They proceeded down the wide main aisle. The columns she had originally thought were random did have a pattern. They were aligned in curving rows branching off the main aisle. Some were short, but more were tall. She took a detour.

"What are you doing?" Blackie crouched beside her. He'd stayed in human form this time.

"I want to figure out what these are, and maybe why some are different sized." Linn pulled out her pocket knife and scraped off the frost.

"But..." He started.

"No." Linn hit something metal, and chiseled off a lump of ice. "Black metal. Like the one over by the small room, but frosty. The short ones aren't frosty. Why?"

Blackie didn't answer, and she stood up and started to chip at the top.

"I'm not running into the problem, this time. I need to know what this place is, and why we're here."

"Shouldn't you be following your feather?" He pulled out a bigger knife and started to help her, and Merrick joined on the other side. Linn smiled down at the ice. He was giving in.

"When I see..." Linn felt the ice she was chipping at loosen, and with almost numb fingers, she lifted it away.

"Holy..." Merrick bit off whatever he was going to say. Linn just gasped, and Blackie was silent. They all stared at the face in the coffin.

It was still, calm, and very pale. A sheet of what looked like glass formed the top of the box he laid in.

"I wonder who he is... was." Linn said finally.

"I think I know where the glass coffin came from in Sleeping Beauty." Blackie murmured.

"What about the glass slipper?" Merrick asked.

Linn shot him a dirty look. This was no time for a joke. "That's a mistranslation. It's a fur slipper."

She turned away from the man in the glass coffin and kept walking into the mist. Merrick caught up with her. "No glass? my childhood fantasies are shattered."

Linn snorted. "Maybe it had glass beading."

"Just what is this place?" Blackie was looking all over at once, a sign he was spooked.

"Cryostasis." Merrick and Linn said it at the same time.

"Jinx." He grinned at her. She rolled her eyes, but let him talk. "Frozen and sleeping, would explain why Mac'Lir said he had been asleep, not just gone."

Blackie nodded. Linn held up her hand for them to stop and shut up. They silenced immediately, and she smiled a little. She had them well-trained already. She listened hard. Silence. She became aware that she could actually hear their hearts beating, over her own.

"Um." Linn took a deep breath. "I think that overdose made everything more... more."

"What?" Merrick sounded confused.

Linn explained as they walked, about the room, and being drunk on power when she came out. "I think it's still affecting me. I can hear heartbeats."

"Oh, is that all?" Merrick flashed a grin at her. "I can do that when I'm a wolf."

Linn stuck her tongue out at him. Her eyes on Merrick, she missed what Blackie saw. "Hey, look at this!"

He'd swerved off the main aisle and was standing next to one of the columns. It was defrosted, and the lid was off, leaned up against it. "Maybe this is the one Mac'Lir was in."

"It's the only one we've seen that isn't operational." Merrick agreed, looking inside it. Linn was looking at one of the other coffins.

"Guys..." She breathed, finally, getting their attention away from the empty column. They came to see what she was looking at. The frost on this column was disturbed, almost the entire top cleared, with delicate crystals reforming over the glass. They didn't obscure the face of the beautiful girl inside, though. She was almost Linn's age, Linn decided, although with an immortal, appearances could be deceiving. She lay on her side, like she was sleeping, wrapped in a blue cloak like she had lain down for a nap. Her blonde hair cascaded around her.

"I thought Snow White had black hair?" Blackie broke the long silence.

"Sleeping Beauty was blonde." Linn muttered.

"Neither. This must be Niamh of the Fair Hair." Merrick took a half-step back. "Look."

He pointed, and it took Linn a moment to realize what he was showing them. There were deep grooves in the frost that had accumulated around the base, and blood, in the grooves and droplets of it scattered and frozen into the ice.

"He tried to get her out and couldn't." Merrick whispered, and Linn knew he was seeing it in his mind's eye, Mac'Lir clawing desperately at the icy coffin, trying to awaken Niamh and release her. She put her hand on his shoulder. His face was showing how shaken he felt at that mental image.

"So now we know why he sent us." Linn wasn't sure they would be able to succeed, but this was definitely technology, and she had done all right so far.

Merrick shook his head. "No."

"What? You don't want to get her out?" Linn was confused.

"I mean this isn't why he sent us. What does your feather say?" Merrick took her hand and looked at it. The mark was as bright as it had been.

"I don't really know. Maybe since I OD'd on the power? It's been bright since I woke up after that." Linn was sure it hadn't been that bright before.

"Move around. Does it still tug at you? I'm sure he wouldn't have sent us, and said it was to save the world, if it was for his daughter. Not Mac'Lir." Merrick nudged Linn back toward the main aisle, chivvying her away from Niamh like a sheepdog more than a wolf.

"All right, all right, I'm going." Linn had to admit she did feel it, still tugging toward the depths of the mist. She looked back toward Niamh's coffin. They'd come back. She wasn't about to leave Mac'Lir's daughter, with his blood showing how hard he'd tried to get her out. Blackie caught up, and the three of them kept going.

The room widened, Linn thought, or the mist got thicker, it was hard to tell. She wondered, given the Sanctuary library shape, that of an eye. Maybe the beings called gods liked symbolic shapes? This could be a leaf, with the columns forming veins. She started to feel like she could see movement in the mist. It was making her jumpy, and she wasn't the only one. They were walking in a tight group, now, and when Merrick stopped abruptly, pointing, she jumped.

"Look at that." He led the way to the column. It was lumpy, unlike all the others, with something poking up from the top. Linn could see when they got near that it wasn't in the coffin, or on it, but leaning up against it. A spear, with a leaf-shaped head, and under the frost, other things, although it was hard to make them out, white with the slow ice-build up.

Blackie pulled his pack out and started rummaging in it.

"What are you doing?" Linn asked curiously.

"Hang on... Aha!" He held up a small hatchet triumphantly. "This will be quicker than pocket knives and fingers.

"Wait!" Linn jumped toward him, but he had already swung full force, with the hammer side of the tool downward.

He was right, it did work better than the knives. The ice cracked, and some slid off at his feet.

"You idi-" Linn strangled her anger and lowered her voice from the shout. "You could have broken it. You might have killed whoever is in there. What were you thinking?"

She would have said more, but he wasn't listening to her. He was standing very still, looking over her shoulder at the coffin. She'd pushed in-between him and it, before he could hit it again.

"What is it? Is something waking up and coming after me?" Linn was unnerved by the look on his face. Blackie shook his head.

Merrick spoke. "I think you ought to look at this, Linn."

She turned around and looked down, into the face of a man she had never met. Gray, grizzled, with a beard that reached down to the hands folded over a small potbelly. But the significant feature was the leather eye-patch over one eye, with scarring showing as a clue to what did... or didn't... lie behind it.

"Odin." Blackie breathed, finally breaking from his trance. He stepped close, next to Linn. Leaning over the glass, he put his hand on it, over the tranquil face. "This is... this is *fimbulwinter*."

"That was a legend. About the whole earth, and the reign of the ice giants-" Linn broke off. This was a cold place, of ice, and sleep... Maybe he was right.

Blackie looked around. "They are all here, then."

"Most likely." Linn looked at the rows of coffin columns. "All the gods who grew tired of life, retreated here, to sleep."

"I wonder if they dream." Merrick, standing on the other side, mused, looking down into the Norse god's face.

Linn opened her mouth to say something about being frozen, and then closed it again. She knew the immortals were different. Just how different, she wasn't entirely sure.

"We need to keep going," she finally said, "this isn't quite it."

She was sure they were close, though. They returned to the main aisle, and when she moved, Linn could feel the tugging get stronger. She also started to see flickers out of the corner of her eyes, movements in the mist. That had stopped while they looked at Odin, she was sure. Was something following them, or was the slow movement of the fog around them playing tricks with her head?

Silently, they walked on. Linn turned her head to look behind them, and couldn't see the far side of the room any longer. They were surrounded by the mist. She thought it was beginning to get brighter in front of them, though. She shivered, and then wondered if that was the chill, or tension.

It was much brighter, now, and she could see that there were lights, framing an archway. It wasn't, they discovered as they walked up to it, in the wall of the room. Instead, it gleamed in solitary splendor, as they discovered, circling it.

"This is it." Linn looked at her hand. It was back to being a faint glow, now they had reached their destination.

"What is it?" Blackie looked up. The top of the arch was just to the roof of the room. The fog seemed to hold back from it, leaving them standing in a circular open space, but Linn couldn't feel any breeze.

"I think it's a doorway." Linn had noticed that none of them seemed inclined to walk through the arch. Blackie and Merrick had followed her lead in walking around it.

"A doorway to where? The high plane?"

Linn shook her head, getting closer to one of the legs of the arch. It was made of smooth metal, she thought, with an iridescent finish, and no markings at all. Tentatively, she reached out to touch it. It was warm, she thought, surprised, resting her whole hand on it. When it lit up, she jumped backward in surprise.

Slowly, symbols she knew from the computer and machine screens glowed to life on the arch, until the whole thing was alive with energy. It was vibrating, and she backed away, finding Blackie and Merrick right with her. She stopped at the edge of the mist, and watched as the empty air in the archway shimmered. Like a curtain, golden lights spilled from the top of the arch to the floor, shimmering. Then an image appeared.

"It's a holograph." Blackie said, taking a step forward. "How cool."

The image was pretty amazing, Linn had to admit. A dragon's head, metallic brown, the one eye showing closed, his chin resting on the floor as though he were asleep. Had it been real, on the other side of the arch, it could not have fit through it. The dragon's skull was too big. Linn had a flash of insight.

"Oh."

Merrick looked at her. "What is it?"

"Hang on a minute." Linn walked back to the arch and knelt, looking for something. Failing to find it, she walked around the back, seeing the same image as the front. Perhaps the front was the back? Hard to tell orientation, but the back wall of the room was only ten feet behind her, with no columns to block movement through the arch, if it were a doorway, so this could well have been the front. At the other leg, she repeated her search. Merrick was right on her heels. Blackie was on the other side, for all she knew staring at the dragon still.

"What are you looking for? I could help look." Merrick offered.

"No... I need you to keep an eye out." Linn bent down. It was hard to make out the metal surface with the lit symbols on it. She wasn't sure touching it would shut it back down, and didn't want to try, lest she start something.

"For what?" He sounded mystified, but looking up, she could see him turn slightly away from her and start scanning the area.

"Because I'm sure there's something in the fog." She looked back down. Aha!

"You saw that too?" He took a sideways step as she slid the computer case out of the stash place and onto the floor.

"I wasn't entirely sure. But it bothered me." Linn opened the computer and pressed the button. She rocked back on her heels to wait for it to boot. "I'm glad you saw it too."

Blackie, just out of sight, made a noise. Linn jumped up, and Merrick turned just as Blackie walked around the column, looking angry.

The anger would be for the knife-blade to his throat. Held by a tall, thin man dressed in what Linn thought were Norse clothes, the knife pressed at the skin, and Linn could see Blackie was practically on tip-toes to try and keep away from it, his eyes very wide. He didn't dare shift, she guessed, with the threat on him.

Linn took a deep breath, and spread out her hands to her sides, showing them empty. She hoped they didn't look threatening, and was afraid they did, the sturdy Merrick behind her, no doubt glowering over her shoulder.

"Who are you?" Linn broke the silence after a long moment. "And what do you want?"

17

TRICKSTER

he man frowned, his dark brows drawing very close together. Linn wondered how long he had been out of his coffin. There was no place else he could have come from. He spoke in a guttural language.

"I don't understand you. Great. Stuck with a madman and no way to communicate. Blackie, don't move!"

Blackie stopped his wiggle and glared at her. Linn glared back. Then she switched her gaze to the strange man, who had long black hair, tied back, a thin, clean-shaven face, and vivid green eyes. She looked into the eyes for a moment, seeing a flicker of emotion cross his face.

"Let me look at you." Linn, her heart in her throat, closed her eyes. It made her feel somehow out of control to have them closed. Vulnerable, as if he could do anything because she wasn't looking at him. The column beside her gleamed brightly white. Blackie was bright blue, and behind him, was a familiar grass green. She had seen that signature recently.

Confused, Linn opened her eyes. She started to say something, but the man spoke, this time in halting English.

"Who... are you?" He was frowning, but less angry and more thoughtful, she hoped.

"I am Linnea, granddaughter of Hephaestus. That," she pointed toward them, indicating Blackie, "is the son of Sekhmet, Blackie. Behind me," she pointed again – his eyes followed her gestures. She didn't know if he was following all the words – "is Merrick, of Manannan Mac'Lir's Court."

Abruptly, he lowered the knife. Blackie stumbled forward, onto hands and knees, and Linn knew what he was thinking.

She lunged forward to grab him, as he shifted to cat. "No!"

The man leaped backward, an expression of surprise on his face, and Linn wrestled with a very large and angry black cat on the floor.

"Stop it! We don't know he's an enemy; he didn't hurt you, did he?"

She wound up with her arms and legs wrapped around him, and Blackie lay still. He could have gotten her off him easily, and they both knew it, but she'd never done this before. It must have caught him by surprise, she thought. She touched the fur at his neck. "No wounds."

He shook himself all over and got up, leaving her lying on the floor, before he stalked over to sit very erectly next to Merrick, wrapping his tail around his paws and pinning his ears back. Okay, he was not a happy camper. Linn looked up and saw the man step toward her, a hand outstretched. She lifted her own to take it, ignoring the twin growls from behind her.

His hand was warm, and a little damp. They made him nervous, too, she thought, as she got to her feet. While his hand was still on hers, he leaned forward a little.

"I am Loki, Odinsson."

There was a spark of power, and she dropped his hand hastily. Loki was a chancy god, by all the legends. A trickster, like Coyote... she glanced at the arch, which still showed the great sleeping dragon. One of the gods who was a human lover, by all accounts, but...

"Loki," Linn gave him a little bow. "We came, sent by Mac'Lir, to this place not to do harm, but to right a wrong."

Whatever he had done with that power transfer had helped him with the language, she noted as he spoke again.

"Welcome to Hel." He gave her a thin smile, then looked behind her, at the boys. "I am not a threat to you, if you are who you say you are."

Merrick came forward and put a hand on Linn's shoulder. "Daughter of Fire is under my protection."

His presence made Linn feel better, and Blackie silently padding to her other side didn't hurt.

"You fear invaders?" Linn asked Loki, watching his face. He looked troubled.

"I am... uncertain. I was awakened out of time, and with a feeling that aught was ill in this place. So, I was watching, when I saw your party."

The word choices threw Linn for a moment. He meant group, by party, that was archaic, but she understood. She answered him slowly. "How do you awaken a person, in this place?"

He looked away from her. "I... do not know." Loki spoke very slowly, and softly.

Linn wondered who he was worried about, like Mac'Lir's Niamh. "Is anyone else awake?"

He shook his head and looked at her. Linn could see the pain in his eyes. "I am alone. All alone."

Merrick squeezed her shoulder. Linn put her hand up and patted his fingers. "This arch... what is it?" she asked Loki.

He looked at it, bewilderment on his expressive face. "I'm not sure, only that it is of great power, and very important. Why?" He muttered that last word, pacing toward it.

"Be careful!" Linn called as he stuck his hand out toward the shimmering holograph.

He jerked his hand back, and put a finger in his mouth. "It bit me."

She sighed. "No, I think it shocked you. Feel the air, here? How it shimmers a little, and makes the hair on your arms stand up?"

He nodded, shoving back a long sleeve and revealing a very pale arm with fine dark hairs on it. Loki studied the hairs intently.

"That's electricity, and it's dangerous." Linn explained.

"You touched it?" Loki asked, looking at each of them. Linn shook her head.

"You knew." He focused back on Linn again, and walked up close. Linn could feel Merrick's fingers grip her tighter as Loki neared them. "I know the Artificer. You have some look of him. So perhaps you do know."

Linn shook her head. "I have no idea. And I think it's time I admitted that, and called in Grandpa Heff."

She looked at the image again. "Or someone else. As soon as I saw the dragon, I knew what I had to do."

Linn looked Loki in the eye. "Will you trust me?"

He blinked. "I trust no one, child. Why you?"

"Why not?" Linn shot back at him, daring, and hoping what the legends said about his sense of humor was accurate.

Loki threw back his head and laughed. "Why not, indeed? How long have I slept?"

Linn thought about it. "Since possibly 1100 AD I'd think. So... a thousand years, give or take a few decades."

She was basing her guess off Mac'Lir's retirement from his beloved Isle of Man with the coming of Christianity. The Vikings had converted about then, too...

Loki smiled, his face lighting up with his humor. "So little time, then? I had thought an age had passed."

"It has. Humans have progressed faster in the last hundred years than at any point in history."

Now, she had surprised him. His mouth dropped open. "Have the Olympiads fallen, then? To lose their grip on man?"

"Not entirely. But there are those who fight them, to see humanity rise and walk on their own, free men."

Loki eyed her speculatively. "You are one of those fighters."

"We are." Linn carefully included the boys in her rejoinder. Loki had mostly been ignoring them. She held his gaze. "I ask again, will you trust me?"

Loki took her completely by surprise, and went down on one knee before her. In this position, his eyes were on a level with hers. He was not, she thought, trying to show submission, but...

"Little Daughter of Fire, I will follow your lead in this matter, will that suffice?"

His breath was warm on her face, slightly spice scented. Incongruously, Linn wondered how he had been eating in this barren room. She answered, "It is enough."

"Then, what would you have of me?" Loki held this pose perfectly. He'd towered over her, but now they were nose to nose, and his green eyes were deep enough to fall into. Linn took a deep breath, feeling the reassuring grip of Merrick's hand. He'd keep her from falling, she knew that.

"Will you leave this place, for a short time," Linn hastened to add, "And come with me? I think I know someone who has answers."

Again, she looked at the dragon, and he followed her gaze. Neither spoke for a few moments. Then Loki met her eyes again, before looking up at Merrick, over her shoulder, then at Blackie. With his silent assessment over, and Linn would have given much to know what he was thinking of them, he locked eyes with her. She felt that odd sensation again.

"I am at your service, Lady." Loki bent his head slightly, so they were almost touching, and then stood, a little smile on his lips. "Lead on!"

The walk back didn't take nearly as long as they had, coming in. Linn discovered that whatever she had done to the ventilation was working. They came out of the fog bank into a more-or-less clear room, and could see from wall to wall. It did, she noted, narrow to a point at the tunnel, with small shoulders flaring out there, like a leaf. She wondered if the whole room would be clear of mist when they returned. This shouldn't take long.

Loki, pacing beside her while the boys were a few steps behind them, was silent, but looking in all directions, his eyes sharp. She didn't think he missed anything, especially when she looked at the coffin of Niamh as they passed it, even if she didn't slow down or go over to it. Linn remembered something.

"When did you wake up?" She looked at him sideways, without slowing her pace. He was long-legged enough she wasn't rushing him.

"I'm not sure... Less than a day," he said. "I have neither eaten nor drunk since I wakened, but I am not weak."

Linn blinked. "Hang on."

She wasn't sure how he would react, but he didn't at all, to her pack appearing from thin air. Evidently, he knew that trick. He was politely dubious about the protein bar and water bottle. She distributed them to the whole group, and he watched the young people start to eat before he did. When he did take a bite, though, he got a pleased look on his face.

Linn remembered that sugar or even honey, would have been a great treat during his time.

They ate standing, and as soon as she was sure all the wrappers were gone, they moved on and quickly were in the tunnel. Loki looked disturbed, and tended to walk close enough to Linn to occasionally bump shoulders with her.

"Are you okay?" Linn asked after the third or fourth time it had happened.

"I am not good with small spaces." Loki admitted.

"Just keep walking. We'll be out soon." Linn looked over her shoulder. Merrick rolled his eyes, and Blackie flattened his ears at her. She knew they weren't happy, but she was absolutely certain this was what she had to do. She'd known it as soon as she glimpsed the dragon on the arch, which they had left fully activated. Linn was afraid to meddle more with it until she had a chance to talk with someone.

She didn't stop them again for a break, and as they weren't being cautious this time, it took them much less time to get to the surface of the island, and step through the tingling surge of power that was the doorway. Loki stood in the overcast day, shading his eyes with one hand, and blinking tears from his eyes as the wind and cold hit him. Maybe the smell, too; Linn hadn't gotten the full effect of that before, she'd been concentrating on finding the door.

Linn turned to look at the boys, and then turned back to Loki. "You know the High Path, yes?"

He nodded. "Of course. Valhalla may be reached through it, but it is the coward's way. Is that where we are going?"

Linn shook her head, recalling that Loki was not terribly brave, in the old legends. He'd been to Valhalla, coward's way or not, she'd bet on it. "We're going to Idaho, to visit..." her voice faltered. She wasn't sure if friend was the right word. "Someone I know," she finished weakly.

The boys came back from their little escape into the rocks. "Ready," Merrick reported.

"Then let's go." Linn focused on her destination, and stepped out, and up, into the Path.

They traveled in silence, letting her set the pace. Linn would have been running, if she could, but kept herself to a fast walk. Loki kept up with her easily, as did Merrick, behind them, and Blackie ranged out in front, looping back to her often to touch nose to hand.

"You work well together." Loki observed in a low tone. "Your men are obviously well trained."

Linn giggled. "Not my men. Blackie and I have been friends since he was a kitten, and I met Merrick," she looked over her shoulder and raised her voice so she was sure he could hear. "We met less than a week ago, right?"

"More, if you count the days you were unconscious after the battle." Merrick sped up a bit until he was on her other side.

Loki did look startled, now. "You are a shield-maiden?"

Linn shrugged, uncomfortable. "I just did what seemed like the right thing to do at the time." She looked at Merrick.

"Do you know what happened to Lambent?" she asked him.

"Lambent?" Merrick's brown eyes met hers, and she could read the concern in them. He really didn't trust Loki.

"My sword. Last I saw it, was stuck in a troll's neck." Linn wasn't sure he'd been in any better shape than she was at that point in the fight.

Merrick shook his head. "I don't know. We can ask Mac'Lir when we return."

"We are not going to Mac'Lir now?" Loki broke into their conversation.

"No," Linn answered. "He's on the High Plane. What you might know as the *sidhe*."

"Ah." Loki fell quiet again, his face brooding.

Linn felt the path slope downward. It was not, she had figured out, an actual slope, but the way the corridor let those who were traveling it know they were nearing their destination. Linn took a deep breath. She hadn't seen this person for two years, and she wasn't sure they would get a straight answer. Or any answer at all.

Time to get down to Earth again. She stepped out of the Path, and onto a sunlit bed of pine needles, which crunched a little underfoot. There was faint rutting, and it was hard to tell this dirt road was traveled at all, but Linn had been here before. Loki was looking around, wide eyed, along with Merrick. She had to guess they had never seen the wide skies and tall pine trees, the crisp dry air, and the intoxicating scent... Linn drew in a deep breath, smelling it. She'd missed that.

"Blackie?" Linn called him from where he'd been stalking a mouse, it looked like. He cocked his head at her. "Do you remember where we are?"

The big cat swung his head from side to side. He had been a kitten when she had carried them here, tucked in saddlebags, believing Patch and Moira dead in the cabin explosion. Linn nodded. She hadn't expected, but then, he wasn't normal.

Linn led the way down the faint track through the woods, walking on a golden carpet of fallen needles and enjoying the smells of the forest, the feel of the sun on her face. She wasn't sure when they would meet who they had come for, but she was sure he was home. He was always home.

18

HUNTING

*L*inn paused, holding up a hand for the boys to stop. Loki stepped up beside her and asked "What is it?"

"Listen." She wasn't sure what it was, but she'd heard something. There were elk in the woods, bears, mountain lions. It could have even been one of the ubiquitous rabbits, but this rustling had been... larger.

"I'm not hearing anything." Loki spoke again.

Out of the corner of her eye, Linn could see Blackie ghosting off between the trees, and then a silvery-gray flicker of movement. She turned her head. Merrick had gone... that was him, then, back in wolf-form and hunting. They had heard it too.

"Let's keep going, then." Linn was a bit irritated with Loki. He was supposed to be a sneaky one, and he seemed to be oblivious to his surroundings out here. In the underground room, he'd been on edge. Now, he was acting all fat and happy.

"We're on Earth." Loki said now.

Linn didn't look at him. Why was he acting all stupid? "Yes, we are."

"I thought we were traveling to the High Plane, as you term it."

"No, I said Mac'Lir was there. Not that we were going there." She glanced at him, wondering if something was wrong.

"Who are we going to see, then?" He was looking straight ahead, walking casually, like they were strolling in a park.

"Someone who may have the answers." Linn really wished he would be quiet so she could listen.

"You are being very coy, m'dear." Loki looked down at her and smiled.

Linn felt faintly nauseated at the look on his face. She bit back her first thought, which was to snap back that she was not a child.

"I don't know if he will talk to us." She also didn't know his name, and thought his nickname was probably not a good idea to share.

"You don't know... then why did we come all this way, and in such a hurry?" Loki had stopped and was staring at her.

"Because while I'm not sure he'll talk to you, I'm fairly certain he will speak to me." Linn kept walking. She didn't know it for sure, but he'd been welcoming, two years before, and she was sure that time meant little to this being.

"Little Spark..." The deep voice rattled her bones, but she hadn't heard it with her ears.

"Monster." Linn responded, speaking out loud to the thin air. "I have come with questions."

"And companions." The voice was velvety, but powerful enough that she had always felt he kept it dialed back for her. Like the full voice would do damage to her frail human side. "Such interesting minds you bring me, Bright Spark."

Linn was amused. Another name to keep track of. What was it with the gods and names?

The Monster answered her unspoken question. "Names are significant, and private. Descriptive names work just as well, and Bright Spark suits your mind, child."

Linn got a vivid mental image of huge, taloned fingers cupping a little girl, and a puff of hot breath blown over the girl made her flare like a candle with power. "I had a little too much..."

She was thinking of the underground room, and the power in it. He chuckled in her head. "I meant when you were here before, and I ignited you."

"Oh." Linn didn't mind the Monster thinking of her as a child. To him, even Coyote was a brash young man, and Coyote was impossibly old, even for the ever-living. She thought of Granny Clinch.

"What a fast mind, and so cluttered right now." Monster mused. She felt like he was standing, looking over her shoulder as all her memories flickered by on a screen she was looking at. He was manipulating her thoughts, and reading her mind. Now, Linn did feel a flash of fear and resentment.

"No, child. I only read what you give me the images for. You have free will, and can put me out of your mind altogether, should you want to."

She felt him withdraw, and blinked at the sudden emptiness and loneliness. Linn looked around. All three of the men were gathered around her.

"Are you well?" Loki asked. The others, in beast form, couldn't speak but she could see they were worried as well.

"What happened?" Linn asked.

"You stopped, stock still, and stared into - nothingness." Loki explained.

"Oh..." She'd thought they would have heard her side of the conversation with Monster, but evidently not. "Our host is waiting, just on the other side of the hill..." She pointed. Loki gave her a very odd look, but followed when she started walking again.

She let them all get a little ahead. She wanted to see their reaction to Monster's Valley. There was a slight rise in the road, then it got steep enough to make them scramble, and on the peak of the pass between hills, they stopped, the three of them, staring at what lay below. Linn had seen it before, the utter desolation of black ashes, rustling in the wind, but never quite blowing away. The great white bones, their covering of scales and flesh long gone. The huge skull, vacant eye sockets looking straight at the access road. Monster was long dead.

The spirit of the dragon lived on, though. He was alone, having warded his valley so no human gaze would ever see it. Only his friend Coyote came on a regular basis, and had even made a house of sorts, where Linn had visited before. Now, she could hear the scales hissing over stone as the Monster came toward them.

She could see on their faces the alarm, and mixed with fascination on

Loki's part as the illusion of the living dragon slithered up. Deep bronze and browns, the dragon looked much like he had in the holograph deep below the Icelandic volcano.

"Welcome, children." Now, she was sure, they all heard him, the ground shaking a little. He wasn't being quiet. He meant to impress on... Loki, she was sure, that he was there, and more powerful than the little god.

"May we enter?" Linn asked. She knew that even in death, the Monster had formidable defenses.

"Come, refresh yourselves, and tell me why you have come."

The illusion turned his head away from them, and slid smoothly away, leaving a clear path that stretched across the valley to the vast skull. The ash was gritty to walk on. Every so often, Linn caught a glimpse of the metallic scales: buried in the ash, but revealed in tantalizing flickers of light as the restless wind moved the ashes. The path followed the curve of the bones, up and around from the tail, under the high arch of the rib cage, the bleached bone overhead eerily similar to the metal arch she had awakened.

She was thinking, as fast as she could, about everything that had happened, from the beach at Sanctuary, up until now. She knew it was probably muddled, she kept forgetting things in the story and jumping back and forth, but the Dragon's quiet purr of amusement in her head reassured her. Of all the people she knew, he'd be able to keep up with this torrent of information.

She wrapped it up with the image that had brought her here, when there was no time, and she was afraid, and–

"Hush, Bright Spark." He was soothing, and she felt like he'd wrapped her up in a gentle hug. "Do not fret. You have come for answers, and I will give them freely. But before we talk, I will play host. Enter, and find refreshments."

They had reached the skull, while Linn walked along half in a trance telling her story. Blackie and Merrick both sat at the foot of the rickety staircase, staring upward. Merrick wagged the tip of his tail as she walked up to them. She was tempted to pat his head, and decided she'd better not.

They weren't about to try the stairs without her, she realized. Linn walked past them and up the stairs, which weren't, quite, as rickety as they looked. She could feel them following her, for instance. She also knew without having to look that Loki was behind her, and then the boys.

Loki had gotten very quiet since he'd met Monster. She wondered if he was having an internal conversation of his own.

"No," Monster said quietly. "He is worried about me. He cannot quite remember me, but the legends of the past are bright in his mind, as he seeks an answer."

"Is he dangerous?" Linn had been sure of that, when she first saw him holding Blackie, but then he was very stupid in the forest... Monster chuckled.

"He is very dangerous. He was trying to trick you into talking, child, he sees you as an infant in arms, and also as a woman whose head he can turn."

Linn was revolted. "I'm not-"

"You aren't." Monster agreed. "You are very young, and you have not blossomed into full womanhood, but you are a Bright Spark, and he did not see that."

Linn decided she wasn't going to ask about Blackie and Merrick; that felt like invading their privacy. She had needed to know about Loki, though, because it looked like she was stuck with him. She didn't trust him out of her sight, in that room, and here...

"I watch." Monster's voice was serene. "Enter."

The door in the eye socket wasn't round, it was framed in to allow them to enter where the ocular nerve had penetrated to the brain. Loki had to stoop more than a little to get in, and Linn had to bend her head a little. She hadn't, on her last visit.

Linn looked around the room. It hadn't changed since then. It was mostly one large, open room, a floor laid into the brain case to give a living space, and she knew there was a small stable beneath them, from her last time. There was a bathroom, which she pointed out to the newcomers, and watched all three make a beeline for it. She turned to look at the table, which was set for five.

"Who else is coming?" She asked Monster.

"You will see," His voice was warm with amusement.

Out of the corner of her eye she could see Loki come out of the necessary room, and stop to look at the bookshelves. Linn went to stand next to him.

"Coyote prefers moderns." She told him. "Mostly fiction."

"Coyote lives here?" Loki looked alarmed.

"Yes, part time. He'd rather be out in the wild, but this gives him a home, and he keeps Monster company." Linn looked up at him. "You know Coyote."

It didn't quite come out a question. She was certain he did.

"I know him, yes. We have had... disagreements." Loki glanced toward the door as though he expected Coyote to walk through it, and to be unhappy with his presence in Coyote's home.

"He's busy." Linn didn't explain more than that. She wasn't going to trust the Norse god, she'd decided a while back, even if she had asked him for trust.

Loki looked relieved. Linn wondered if that was a story she wanted to know, or not. Behind her, the door opened, and she turned to look.

"Grandpa!" Linn shouted as she ran toward the barrel-chested man who had walked through the door. He held out his arms for her and hugged her tight.

After a long minute, he pushed her away a little, still holding onto her upper arms. "Let me look at you."

She could see in his eyes that her appearance was making him unhappy. "I'm ok. Really, I am."

He nodded. "Your Mom said you were, and she wouldn't have left you if you weren't ready, but still." He stroked her cheek. "I'm glad I didn't see you fight, and sad, as well. You're beautiful, child, and the thought of seeing you in battle chills me, but I'm happy you fought like a tiger."

Linn could feel herself blushing. Grandpa Heff let go of her with a last quick hug, and turned to face the other immortal in the room. "Loki," he said, his voice neutral to Linn's ears.

"Hephaestus. Or do you now prefer Vulcan?" Loki inclined his head in greeting slightly. Linn wondered if handshaking was a modern invention.

"That has not changed." Linn watched them. There was an undertone to her grandfather's words, seeming to say that Loki hadn't changed, either. Grandpa Heff looked taller, now, his face fierce and eyes glowing. He held Loki's gaze for a long moment, and then Loki looked away.

"I see the library here is delightfully light hearted." Loki murmured, slipping sideways, and speaking as though he were addressing her grandfather. Linn rather thought he was escaping that eye contact, instead.

Heff looked at her, smiling, and losing the fearsome storminess that had gathered for Loki. "I think you have something to tell me? Monster was most unhelpful with his summons."

"I'm not sure yet." Linn flicked a glance at Loki's back, and saw her grandfather nod just a little. "Where are the boys? We should eat... I'm starving."

Grandpa raised his voice. "Blackie!"

He hadn't met Merrick yet, Linn remembered. It was hard to remember, herself, that they had only known one another for a week. It seemed like they had known one another forever. Both boys popped around the corner in human form, and Grandpa Heff raised an eyebrow. Oh... he hadn't known about that, either.

Blackie got an attack of the shys, Linn saw, as he blushed a little and offered his hand to the old god. Heff laughed. "Glad to see you join the two-leg club, boy."

Heff pulled Blackie into a hug, thumping him on the back. Then he turned to Merrick, holding out his hand. "I hear good things about you, lad."

Merrick pinked. "Um..." He shook hands, but couldn't seem to find any words.

Heff chuckled all the way to the table. "Sit and eat, no point offending Monster."

There was, Linn was unsurprised to see, a salad and a big pot of rabbit stew on the table, and under a clean cloth, flatbreads. It was what they had eaten before, her first visit, and it was just as good, especially as it had been a while since the last real food her group had seen.

They feasted in silence, Loki looking pouty. The boys were intensely focused on the food. Grandpa looked relaxed, but distracted, and Linn guessed he was talking to Monster. She ate in peace, her belly happy with the tasty food.

The sense of urgency that had been riding her had slipped away, somewhere in the walk through the Valley. She'd brought her problem to the Monster, and now...

"Bright Spark." His voice sounded gentle in her head. Looking around the table, she knew only she could hear him. "May I suggest a walk?"

Linn spoke out loud. "Excuse me, I'm going for a little walk... No, Merrick, I'll be fine. Ask Grandpa, this place is safer than anywhere on Earth."

Merrick sat again, glancing at Heff, who nodded a little. Linn put her dishes by the sink and walked out the door, closing it firmly behind her. She'd seen Loki get up, and wanted to make it clear he wasn't to follow her.

Monster kept quiet while she got safely down the stairs, and Linn appreciated that. She could feel his amusement lurking at the edges of her awareness, though.

"Oh, I know they won't fall down, but my knees don't know that." Linn spoke out loud to him.

"You have allowed your unconscious to guide you many times in the last few days, but it is bothering you."

Linn headed for the massive vertebrae. She had stuffed herself with food and wanted to sit and relax, not walk. Perching on a handy spine, flat, hard, and more than long enough for her to sprawl on in the sun, she responded. "I don't believe in magic."

"No more do I. You are correct, this is not magic. There comes a point, though..."

Linn sighed. "Most of my peers when I went to public school walked around in a daze, with a phone plugged into their ear, staring at the screen. Might as well have been zombies. But if they dropped and broke it? All the magic leaked out. They couldn't have fixed their phones, or computers, to save their lives. And that's how I feel now."

"You are an extraordinary child." Monster sounded serious; he wasn't teasing her. She squirmed.

"I have a big vocabulary, and I'm not afraid to use it." Linn decided flippant would be easier than risking a swelled head.

"Indeed. Are you ready for the answers?" Monster sounded diffident, like this wasn't something he wanted to do.

"Monster, if you could have anything, what would you ask for?" Linn draped an arm over her eyes. The sun was bright, even through closed eyelids.

"Oh... ah," She'd caught him by surprise. "I would like to go home." Monster's voice was very small and still, now.

"Why don't you?" Linn asked. He wasn't actually dead, after all.

There was a long, windy sigh, and the ashes stirred and rustled. Linn could feel the breeze cooling her. "May I tell my story? Much will be illuminated, I suspect."

"I'm sorry, I didn't mean to interrupt."

"Curiosity is a gift, do not lose it." Monster's mental smile was back now.

"Once upon a time and very far away," he began.

Linn giggled a little. She stretched out on the spine, her legs hanging over a little, but she was warm and full... Monster went on, and she drifted into his words.

19

MONSTER'S BIRTH

*A*del'eui D'natti hesitated in front of the arch. "Abandon all hope, ye who enter here," he read, then sucked on his front fangs in consternation. When he had been given this assignment, he'd known it was punishment duty. But those were grim words.

Within his mind, a pre-memory of a tiny soft thing with silky black hair and earnest eyes stirred in her sleep, her dreams his memories, but the being who would become the Monster was more concerned with his past present nowness all here, in his last day at home.

Home. Adel looked up into the sky, pleadingly, at the rosy sun, and the smaller white sun which forever chased his lover across this sky. They said his posting had only one, small, yellow sun. And blue skies. Adel shivered. He was going to be very cold, for a long time.

A clash of chains signaled the arrival of his charges. Adel flattened his crest in dismay. So many of them, and such a strange shape they had. Ter'nian, his commander, snaked his way to the head of the line.

"All formed in the fashion of the inhabitants of the world you are going to." He turned his vast red skull and surveyed the line of prisoners with satisfied eyes. The People had learned generations ago how to manipulate the genes of, well, simply everything. They had conquered disease, death, but they could not alter a mind's will. Which was what brought Adel here, miserable.

It could be worse. He could be in one of those flimsy, two-legged, squishy bodies. Instead, he was the warden of the prison planet that had been dubbed Gaia. The arch flashed into life, the pulsing energy making Adel itch right to the tip of his tail.

The prisoners, chained two by two, walked through the shimmering light of the portal to another world, another universe. Ter stropped chins with Adel.

"Don't worry." He slid backward so Adel had room. "It's only a turn of the galaxy. You'll be back before you know it."

Adel slid forward, into the terrible forces that twisted, squeezed, and shredded his very being...

Linn woke up with a scream. Shaking, she sat up and looked at her hands. They were slim, brown, and five fingered. She made a fist. And no talons.

Monster spoke apologetically. "I am sorry. But it seemed the best way to convey the tale in the least amount of time.

Linn gasped for breath. She was having a little trouble wrapping her head around being a human girl again, rather than a terribly alien dragon being. "I know your name." she whispered. She had an inkling of the honor it was.

"Are you ready? I will be more conventional, now."

Linn nodded, taking a deep breath. Her hands were still shaking a little. She pulled her legs up onto the spine and sat with her arms wrapped around her knees, listening.

"We emerged on the other side of the arch, into that room you so recently explored. The technicians who had prepared it lined the room, leaving a central path for my charges and I to walk through. I remember looking down at them and marveling at how delicate and skilled they were, while they flinched away from me, as I could crush them with the least movement.

"I was a terrible warden, you may think. I remained in Nyx, which is the name of the rooms in the pit of the earth, and sent my charges out into the new world to live new lives. They were not allowed to remember who or what they were, and they were not allowed to remember whence they came, beyond Nyx. They all began in one place, but as I learned later, they were restless, and they moved. They warred, and moved further. In time... But that came later."

The Monster huffed a long sigh, and the ashes moved again. "I was miserable. Depressed, alone, and so cold - I would curl up in the volcanoes for as long as I dared leave Nyx at a time, trying to warm myself."

"I noticed that where there had been many technicians, who were of a race I never knew the name of, only that they were tiny, there were now very few. Each time I returned to Nyx, there were less, and then, there were none."

Linn thought of Deirdre, and the coblyns, goblins, brownies, and others she had no name for. "Yes," Monster said. "They were the ones who came before me, to prepare the machines of Nyx. I assumed they were returning home, and Oh! how I envied them. I no longer spoke to them at all, bitterly jealous of their presumed freedom."

"They weren't, though." Linn thought about it. "And they aren't immortal, so they have forgotten?"

"They are very long-lived, by human standard, but not immortal. And I do not think they forgot; I believe they chose to rub it out of their memories. For fear. They were afraid of me, and for good reason."

Monster's voice faltered, and there was a long pause. Linn stretched back out in the sun. She'd have a burn if she wasn't careful.

"There isn't much more pertinent to what you must know." Monster sounded sad, and he was reluctant to continue.

"I will always respect you." Linn told him, thinking of the tales she knew, of how he had come to this valley and a kind of death.

"I thank you for that. The time came when I crouched by the arch in Nyx. Now, my kind continue to grow as long as we live, and I had grown during my time here on earth. I would barely be able to carefully wriggle through the arch and back to my homeworld. It had been a turning of my home galaxy, about a thousand of your years. I was so weary, and longed for the twin suns of home.

"There was no technician to activate the arch, and my claws catch, I am clumsy... for a time I thought that was why I failed. But now, I believe that the problem was on the other side. The arch came to life, and I saw an image of myself, as I had been that last day. I know who made it. My beloved Ter'nian, who must still be waiting for me on the other side."

"What about... your charges?" Linn asked.

Monster replied slowly. "Theirs was a life imprisonment. That is why they were re-shaped into human bodies. Only I, and the technicians, were to return to home."

Linn pondered this. "Why are there people frozen in Nyx?"

"I shall continue. Be not alarmed."

Linn opened her eyes, confused. The heat of the sun fell away and she was in the shade. Over her hovered a filmy veil of dark ashes, held aloft and offering her protection from the sun.

"I detected a certain amount of distress on the cellular level, and intervened." Monster sounded apologetic.

"Thank you." Linn thought it was like holding a parasol over her to keep off the sun, and the veil of ashes reshaped itself to look like a lace parasol. Linn giggled out loud.

Monster sounded like he was smiling again, even though she now knew he couldn't have smiled when he was living. But he had a sense of humor.

"When I discovered that although I could see the image, and feel the power, I still could not activate the portal to go home, I ran mad. I left Nyx and roamed the world, doing things I am ashamed of, two turns later. I was insane with homesickness and loss. This does not absolve me; only explains how I came... here."

Linn nodded. "And it doesn't tell me about the coffins."

"Coffins?" He sounded mystified.

Linn pictured them in her head: the short ones, the tall ones with the glass part holding a frozen being, and finally Niamh, with the bloody marks of her loving father's fingers.

"Cryostasis is a good word, yes." Monster sent her a moving image of a slow thaw and complete restoration of faculties when complete. "It was where my charges could come when life was no longer endurable, to rest, and retreat from immortality. In my form, there is a sort of hibernation, when we have been awake too long, and the memory maintenance is impossible. Resting allows us to build further storage facilities for those memories."

"I don't think the human brain has that capacity." Linn told him.

"No, it does not. I have learned so much, since I came to an end, and rest, here." Monster sighed, and her parasol wavered, then firmed back up. "The beings who are in Nyx chose to come there, for surcease. They remember it as a refuge, not as a prison."

"Why is Niamh trapped, and why did Mac'Lir think the end of the world was coming?"

"Niamh is trapped, by what you tell me, because the machines are malfunctioning. The computer you describe must be one of the diagnostics that the technicians built, I am as mystified as you why it is human compatible. It will reset and repair any of the machines in Nyx, only it may take a great deal of power."

This didn't surprise Linn. The machine room which had overdosed her was a measure of what Nyx needed. The arch, though.

"I found a reset keypad on the arch." She told him.

Monster shuddered. The whole valley shook, with a long moan from the rocks on the ridges high above them. Linn clung to the great angular bone as the ground rolled like the sea.

"I cannot..." His voice sounded far away, and she couldn't feel him. "I must not..."

"Monster!" Linn watched clouds boil up out of the blue sky, lightning cracking from one top of them to another as they towered overhead. The air cooled, and her hairs lifted as the electricity built. She could see Grandpa Heff run out of the skull and start down the stairs.

"Monster, what is wrong?" she shouted, trying to reconnect with him.

"Hope. I cannot hope." His voice was small, and she could barely hear him over the thunder. Her parasol shattered and drifted down. Linn could taste the ashes on her lips. Salty, like tears.

Loki and the boys were coming down the stairs cautiously. The ground still trembled, but nothing like that first quake. Linn's seat had assumed a slant, but she hung on, afraid to let go. Grandpa reached her.

"Tell him!" Linn demanded of Monster. "Tell him what you are, and why you are mourning."

Hephaestus stood stock still, his eyes closed, for an eternal moment. Loki, Merrick, and Blackie reached them, and Linn let go of the bone long enough to hold up an emphatic finger to her lips. She would explain when she could. She didn't know if Loki was one of the original criminals, banished for who knew what manner of crimes from their homeworld to hers. It didn't matter. He would use anything, she was certain.

Right now, what mattered were the technicians, the ill-used, frightened little people who had fled the Monster who was supposed to be their guardian, but were returning with warped memories to destroy his way home. Or to return home themselves, only they had forgotten how to get there.

Linn shuddered. She had been in the mind of Adel, the tender artist and lover who would not harm anyone, and she knew that was what his world was like. They would fall to the rapacious goblins who had been bred like animals for someone's idea of revenge and reparations for long-gone wrongs. She couldn't let it happen, and without Monster, the being who remained when Adel died...

"Adel'eui D'natti died?" Monster's voice whispered in her ear like a tickle.

"Yes." Linn was sure of it. The being who had lost everything had gained friends, a home, and a place where he was safe. "He is gone."

"Then I need not go home?"

"You are home." Linn pictured the skull, Coyote sprawled on the ragged couch. Herself and the kittens, tumbling on the floor on her last visit. Then she changed her thoughts. Herself, Blackie, Spot, Merrick, the other gods' children of her age, sitting on the edges of the raised gardens Coyote had established on the hostile ash, listening to a lecture on advanced genetic manipulation being given by an unseen teacher.

"You want me to teach you." Monster sounded wondering.

"You already have. If humanity can get far enough ahead, we can beat the gods your people inflicted on us." Linn felt his mental wince, and forged ahead. "You can atone for your carelessness, with care."

She closed her eyes, hugged the bone, and waited.

"Family." Monster's voice was contemplative. "I have never had what you would call a family."

She had a confused and confusing impression of soft eggshell, like a turtle's, and blood, and sharp talons and tearing fangs... "Clutches begin thus, and we shrink from it, when we come to an age of reason."

"Sometimes you have to fight." Linn remembered the goblin battle, with all the details of pain, and fear, and aimless rage of the enemy.

"Yes. Sometimes you must fight." Monster sighed, and the clouds began to fray at the edges. "You must fight for me, Bright Spark. I cannot go, and fulfill my duty."

"I can, and I will." Linn unwound her arms from the white bone and stood up, feeling her legs quiver from all the tension she had been under. She spoke out loud again.

"Do you know what we need to do, Grandpa?"

"Yes, I do. And we have to hurry, I need to make phone calls and gather as many who will help as I can."

Heff was already walking away. Merrick and Blackie looked back and forth between them; confusion written on their faces. Loki stood with his hands folded behind his back, a look of boredom carefully affected on his face. Linn looked at him.

"You are going to be very important to this. We need you to end *Fimbulwinter* and take your people to Valhalla."

Loki, she was delighted to discover, could be genuine. He was genuinely shocked, with his mouth hanging open and everything. Linn ran to catch up with her grandfather, laughing. Just before they left the valley, she bent and scooped up a small thing to put in her pocket.

She missed the horses she had ridden when they had visited before. The valley was not big but she had been walking a lot, in the last couple of days. It was starting to catch up with her. There was no cell service in the valley, Heff needed to get just outside, and then he was on the phone, making cryptic orders and arrangements. They'd gotten quite a way up the faint track through the woods, both boys having shifted and chasing one another through the trees. Linn was eyeing Loki with concern: he'd developed a limp, and she suspected blisters. It had been a thousand years since his last stroll, after all.

"Time to go." Heff opened a path and stepped aside, holding it open as Linn walked past him, and waiting until all of them were in before he too stepped onto the path.

"Where are we going?" Loki ventured.

"To pick up a package, and some technicians." Grandpa Heff strode forward. "This won't take long; we aren't very far."

Linn tagged along; glad she wasn't in charge any longer. At least for now.

20

BRAINS, BRAWN, BEAUTY

*T*hey stepped out into a familiar place, at least for Linn. The airport where those visitors to Sanctuary who could not (or would not) use the High Path came to. Linn looked around as they walked through a door, it would appear to anyone watching. It was night, here, and almost no-one was in the airport.

Linn recognized the tall man at the same moment he saw them and started to walk toward them, a small cluster of people trailing in his wake. "Mr. Q!" she called, bouncing toward him for a hug.

She could hardly greet him by his real name in public. Quetzalcoatl in human form was regal, but she'd gotten to know him well enough to feel comfortable treating him like family. And if he was here, this had become a big mission.

He let her go, and looked at the group following her. His wide black eyes narrowed when he saw Loki. Evidently, no one really liked Loki. Grandpa Heff shook hands.

"Is this the team?" There were three people clustered around looking like they were waiting.

"James Copley," Quetzalcoatl gestured to the tall blond man with a military haircut. He shook Heff's hand, and to her surprise, Linn's. Loki and the boys were hanging back, but Linn watched Copley assess them visually as he stepped back to let a short woman with soft brown hair capping her head step forward.

"Hello, I'm Linda Pierce," she shook hands, and Linn watched Quetzalcoatl smiling fondly down at the much shorter woman. "I'm the brains, James is the brawn. Mr. Q is the beauty." She shot an impish grin at him before stepping back next to James.

Heff laughed. "And the other gentleman?"

"This is Marc, the pilot."

Marc nodded at all of them, and looked at Quetzalcoatl. "I need to finish preflight, if you want to leave right away."

"Thank you, Marc."

The man turned and walked away.

"The package?" Heff asked.

Copley answered. "I have it tucked in, all cozy on the plane, sir. When we dust off, I'll be babysitting."

Linda chimed in. "And I will be working on reprogramming. Which I understand you know something about, Linnea?"

Linn nodded. "Will I be traveling in the plane?"

She was asking her grandfather, but Quetzalcoatl answered. "Yes, to Reykjavik. You will be met there, and taken via helicopter the rest of the way."

Linn looked at James and Linda. "Do you have winter gear? It's cold where we are going, inside and out."

"We weren't told where we were going, so I packed everything. Linda sniffed and gave the tall serpent god a mock glare. "I've worked for Mr. Q long enough to know better than to leave anything to chance."

"I'm prepared," Copley chuckled a little at his partner. "Linda did indeed bring everything. I carried most of it down the concourse."

"There was a cart!" she shot back at him.

"What about the boys?" Linn turned to her grandfather and the oddly silent Loki.

"Coming with me. We have a lot of work to do, and we will meet you there, I promise," he glanced at Loki. "We have an obligation to help him awaken his family. The boys and I will be working on that with Loki before you arrive."

Loki's face softened a little, not quite a smile, but perhaps relief at the offered help.

Copley looked at his watch. "Do you have luggage?" He asked Linn.

Linn looked down at herself, and tried not to think about a shower, and clean clothes. Sanctuary was so close, and yet so far. "No, I don't. I'm ready to go."

"Let's git, then."

Linn fell in beside Linda.

"You have such an interesting haircut, dear." Linda offered.

"I, er, didn't intend to have it cut, it was an accident. And I just haven't had time since it happened." Linn touched the long side. She really didn't even think about it, but she must look ridiculous.

"It's rather hip, I think. Sort of like an asymmetrical cut skirt." Linda was walking with a limp, Linn realized.

"Are you all right?" Linn slowed her pace, realizing that James, ahead of them, was not walking as fast as he could, he was in tune with his partner.

"Oh. I'm fine dear. Just a bit gimpy."

It took them a few minutes to get all tucked into seats, as Linda put it, on Mr. Q's jet. Linn, meanwhile, was missing her companions, and trying to figure out just how much she needed to tell the two humans, and how little she could get away with.

Marc walked into the cabin. "All ready?"

James nodded to him, and Marc tossed him a mock salute before disappearing back to the cockpit. "And now we fly." James settled back and closed his eyes.

"He hates flying," Linda leaned over and confided in Linn. "Tries to sleep through it."

"I manage, too, if you stop talking." The big man retorted without opening his eyes.

Linn yawned; this talk of sleep reminding her how long it had been since she'd last had any. She felt a faint bump as the landing gear retracted. "That was fast."

"It's going to be a long flight, and we have lots of time. Sleep, dear." Linda patted her hand, and Linn stretched her legs out, grateful for the full recliners the Mayan god kept on his luxury jet. She closed her eyes and let the rumble of the jets soothe her to sleep.

She woke up to the smell of food and coffee.

"We're making a refueling stop in an hour, so time to eat before that. After, you and I must work." Linda handed her a mug of steaming coffee.

"Thanks," Linn inhaled. "Mmm!"

"You like coffee?" Linda settled back into her seat. James was out of sight, in the tiny galley, Linn guessed.

"Not really, but after this last week, yes."

"Oh, that bad, was it?"

James came out of the galley with two plates. "Ladies, behold the fine cuisine of the airways, a la James."

He presented them with a flourish and a grin. Linn laughed.

"Thanks..." She took the plate, which had a bagel, fruit, and scrambled eggs on it. "Smells wonderful, meals for me have been erratic recently."

"I'm only sorry there is no bacon," he said.

Linn ate, helped with dishes, and buckled in as the plane descended. She thought they were somewhere on the East coast, but Marc didn't say, and they didn't leave the plane during the hour they were on the ground.

After takeoff, Linda pulled out a laptop. "Let's talk tech, Linn."

They had been chattering about everything and anything, except what Linn had been up to, and what the mission was. It had been fun, and James' dry sense of humor had set Linn off as often as Linda's silly repartee had. Now, Linn sobered up.

"The package, as James called it when we met, needs to be reprogrammed with a time delay. I was a little surprised Grandpa Heff didn't use the team that, er, built it in the first place, for this mission."

Linda nodded. "I think it was because of the transport. We are far less conspicuous than some of his, ah, technical team."

Linn understood. The coblyns, at between three to four feet tall, and green, would stand out like a sore thumb in any airport.

"Then you have consulted with them." Linda nodded, and Linn sighed with relief.

"Will you need to be with the package after the reprogramming?" She asked next.

"Yes, I can't activate and program it until transport is over. It wasn't intended to be moved; you know?"

Linn nodded. It had been created from a carefully hidden 'military-surplus' NIKE missile, and was supposed to be a last line of defense for the Sanctuary itself. Fortunately, it wasn't needed at that time. Now, it was the only way to make sure the portal to another world was closed, and remained closed.

"How long a delay will you need?" Linda asked, tapping away at her program.

"From activation until it goes off?" Linn thought about how long it took to get all the way back to the surface. "Two, maybe three hours?"

"Allowing for some wiggle room?" Linda looked thoughtful.

"Yes, I think so." Linn thought about it. "I don't want to leave too much. There are reasons..."

Linda nodded. "It won't take me long to input this, once we have it in place. All told, maybe fifteen minutes, to double check after installation."

"That shouldn't be a problem." Linn was sure they could do this before the goblin army could figure out where the island was, let alone how to get there. She hadn't seen much sign of intelligence in the attack on Mac'Lir's castle.

"Good! We're all ready, then."

In Reykjavik, Linn discovered that Iceland was as cold and windy as the little island. They didn't go inside. A huge black helicopter waited for them, and she got to see the package for the first time in two years. In a matter of speaking, as it was in a wooden crate. James supervised the strapping-down process while Linda showed Linn how to strap into the canvas sling seat.

Compared to the jet, this was bare-bones. Linn found she was a little, no, make that a lot excited. She had never flown in a helicopter before. It rattled more than a plane.

Also, it was too loud to talk. She looked out the window, finding the ocean a lot closer than she had expected under them. It was the stormy grey-green of Mac'Lir's eyes. Every now and then, there was a froth of white as a wave peaked. The ocean was vast, she knew, and the chances of seeing anything other than water slim. Until she saw something.

Linn leaned as close to the window as she could get. Peering into the water didn't help much. The water wasn't the clear window into the depths she was accustomed to from Hawaii. Here, it was opaque, with the glimpses of something below the surface elusive. Still, she was sure she had seen something.

It took her too long to remember and try her sight on it. Closing her eyes, Linn leaned back on the taut fabric of her seat, and focused downward, on the sea. There were little flickers... she still wasn't sure. Had she ever looked at a lot of water before? No, and she had never looked for the friendly naiads who considered themselves Heff's family, and visited Hawaii often.

She knew that not all the denizens of the ocean considered themselves friendly to humans. Linn wasn't sure if the goblins had allies, and she wasn't sure, now that it occurred to her, where the sea dwellers had come from. Adel's memories had been of humans, and the tiny green technicians.

However, beast forms and shape-shifters, they were all possible with the power of the molecular manipulation that Adel's people had left in the hands of their exiles. Which was where the sea dwellers must have been born. And, if they had hidden in the ocean to get away from humans, maybe some of them had allied with the Olympians, or the goblins.

Linn opened her eyes. Grandpa Heff would be at the island, he would know what to do. There was nothing she could do, until she was on the ground again, anyway. Linn felt twitchy. James was frowning at her. Not like he was mad, but worried. Linn smiled with an effort and made the OK symbol with her hand. He relaxed a little and looked out the window. Linda just had her eyes closed really tight. Linn didn't think she liked flying in the big chopper.

Linn felt the descent start. Now, the ocean was alarmingly near the belly of the chopper. She stopped looking out the window, staring at the ceiling for the time. Helicopters, she discovered, landed harder than airplanes. At least it let her know when it was time to get out. She fumbled at her latches, and James was unstrapping the package. Linda reached over, back to her usual self, and helped Linn out. Linn hopped out of the chopper and kept her head down, as the blades were still spinning.

Between the debris in the air, and the cold, her eyes were streaming with tears by the time she felt like she had gone far enough. She wiped her eyes on her coat sleeve.

When she could see, she gaped in surprise at the scene in front of her. The doorway to Nyx gaped open, white light spilling out onto the rough black scree of the island. Clouds of disturbed seabirds swirled overhead, screaming with anger at the people who were invading their peace. And people everywhere. Linn recognized a few, including Blackie and Merrick who were trotting toward her, or rather, the helicopter. Five men converged on the chopper and James, and with a rope sling, they picked up the package and moved it toward the tunnel.

Linda came up and clutched Linn's arm. "Oh, the footing is horrible here!"

Linn jolted out of her amazed reverie and started helping Linda toward the tunnel mouth. "Lean on me; it's better inside."

"Linn, Heff said he'd see you by the arch," Blackie called as they passed her. Linn nodded, trying to make sure Linda didn't fall.

There was a trickle of people coming out of the door and stepping into a shimmering patch of grayness that was an anchored High Path portal, Linn realized. She didn't know that could even be done for any length of time. Loki was standing by the doorway, speaking to the emerging people, who were mostly dressed as he was, and gesturing them onward to the portal. He met Linn's eyes, nodded, and then smiled.

The sweetness of the smile surprised her.

"Are you well?" He asked her as they reached the doorway.

"I am." She wasn't sure what to make of him.

"I am getting my family to safety." He glanced into the tunnel. The next arrivals were just in sight. "Thank you, Daughter of Fire, for this."

"What?" Linn was startled. He sounded sincere, but then again, he had before.

"I was lonely, and they had lost hope. We had all turned on one another, time and again. Then you came along. What I have seen, through your eyes and visiting those who remained awake and in the world, has given me hope." He shrugged. "Might be that nothing will change. But it could, and there could be a place for children, again."

Linn wasn't sure how to interpret this. "I hope you all happiness." She nodded again, and tugged Linda into the tunnel.

"Dare I ask?" Linda had been silent up until now.

"You know who Loki is?" Linn asked.

Linda nodded. "In the Norse pantheon, he's the one who subverts everything."

"That was Loki." Linn didn't look back, but Linda did, with a comical look of surprise.

"He called you Daughter of Fire?" Linda asked after a while.

"My mother, grandfather, and grandmother are all connected to volcanoes. I'm pretty sure that's where it comes from, I haven't yet asked the people who call me that."

There were two worlds, Linn mused, and the customs were very different on both of them. The High Plane, where the immortals dwelled, and the Earth she had been born and raised on. Now, she seemed to have one foot on each place. It wasn't always a comfortable feeling.

They kept walking, pausing from time to time for Linda to rest. "I have a degenerated hip joint," she told Linn on one of these breaks. "It's better some days, and this is a good day, or I couldn't walk at all."

Linn frowned, and looked at the curve of the walls. She knew they weren't halfway to Nyx, and she really needed to talk to Heff. "May I help?"

"Oh, I don't know how you could. I can't take medications right now, they make me all fuzzy-brained."

Linn held both her hands over Linda's hip area, closed her eyes, and focused. She probably shouldn't be doing this, and was going to get in trouble, but she needed more speed, and she liked Linda. The power sparked from her to Linda's body, and then back again after a few moments. Linn hadn't tried to transfer power, just gave it instructions and had it work for a bit...

Linda gasped and let go of Linn's arm. "What did you do?"

She took a step away. Linn dropped her hands.

"Did it hurt?"

Linda took another step. Linn asked "Did I scare you?"

"Oh, no, quite the opposite. It doesn't hurt a bit!"

Linda started down the tunnel, walking carefully at first, and then with a much longer and more confident stride. "Oh, my- thank you! How long will this last?"

"I think it ought to be permanent." Linn was pleased at their speed, and the broad grin on Linda's face. Getting in trouble didn't matter as much if she could get that look.

"I'm not going to ask, dear." Linda assured her. "I'm just going to appreciate this."

"Okay."

They shared a conspiratorial smile and kept going.

Linda did stop when they walked into the room, and gaped a little. Linn couldn't blame her. It had changed since she last saw it, too. The mist was gone, and the full size of Nyx was revealed. The people walking toward the tunnel and departure from the island had dwindled as they walked, and now there were just a few left in the vast room. Linn thought she could make out a knot of people at the far tip of the leaf, by the arch, which glowed and shimmered still.

"What was this place?" Linda asked as they walked down the central aisle.

"It's called Nyx," Linn wasn't sure how much more she should say.

"Night? The cave the Titans came from." Linda didn't press Linn for more information, which she was grateful for.

Heff came to greet them. "Linda, thank you for coming, I know this can't have been easy."

Linda gave him her best impish grin. "Linn was such a big help. I'm going to go help James before he drops something."

Linn gave her grandfather a quick hug. "Grandpa, what do naiads look like under water? With the sight, I mean?"

He looked a little startled at her unexpected questions. "Um, not as bright as above, in air, the water diffuses the signature they emit a lot, the deeper they are, the harder to see. What did you see?"

21

MONSTER'S BONE

"*J*'m not sure-" Linn was interrupted by a crash and clatter from the group at the arch.

Heff called over his shoulder, already moving. "Hang on a minute."

Linn followed him. She put a hand in her pocket and fingered the little object she had picked up in Monster's Valley. It was smooth, and warm now with her body heat. She still wasn't certain why she had grabbed it, or what she was going to do with it, but an idea was forming.

James stopped mid-word when he saw her coming, with a faintly guilty look. Linn guessed he had been swearing. The stripped-down missile, revealed by the partial deconstruction of the crate, was gleaming silvery like the last time Linn had seen it. She wasn't sure what was wrong.

"It's not supposed to do that." James pointed at the access hatch he'd opened. Linn peered into it, curious. Inside was a now-familiar keypad, and an LCD panel, lit up and displaying a menu. It looked perfectly normal to Linn, who admittedly hadn't seen many other nuclear weapons to compare this one to.

"Do what?" Heff asked, his tone conveying that he was as mystified as his granddaughter.

"It turned itself on. I didn't turn it on, Linda hasn't touched it yet," she shook her head in agreement. "I don't know why it turned on, and that makes me really, really nervous." James finished, his face serious.

Linn spoke up. "There is a lot of power emanating from that," she indicated the arch. "And the team which set up the original wiring were connected to the people who built this place. I think they may need to be consulted."

Grandpa Heff frowned. "Linn, they won't come here. Their history with this place is bad, they tell me, when they can be persuaded to talk about it at all."

She nodded. "I know, but they may not have a choice. Also..." Linn looked around the hall of Nyx, almost empty now. "It might be good for them. Only I don't know if we have time."

"What do you mean?" She had his full attention now, and a glower. It was a bit scary.

Linn took a deep breath. "I was starting to tell you what I saw on the way here. A lot of water dwellers, on their way here. I know how they feel about cold water, Grandpa, from our naiads. I also know not all the water folk like humans, or the gods. I'm worried."

Heff nodded; his anger not directed at her. "James, Linda, please see if you can reprogram the device. We will evacuate you as soon as it is done."

He looked down at Linn, and put a hand on her shoulder. "You know what you're doing?"

She shook her head. He laughed. "I'm going to chivvy the last stragglers out of here. Keep a watch."

"What about Blackie and Merrick?" Linn asked. They had been hovering with urgency for the last few minutes. She knew they wanted to be doing something, anything.

Heff turned and beckoned them. "Run through and do last checks to make sure we haven't missed anything or anyone. Eight feet are faster than four."

The boys exchanged a glance and ran behind the arch, using it as a screen for their shift. Linn looked at Linda and James, already fast at work, then headed for her abandoned computer case. She had left it sitting next to the arch, ready to plug in, and it was still there. She knelt and booted up the laptop, wondering what the battery life was like on this thing. There was no way of telling, that she had seen.

Before anything else happened, she needed to do this. There might never be another chance, if the people on the other side reacted the way she thought they would. The Monster hadn't asked, but she had felt Adel's heartbreak and longing. She knew that she would want home, if she were exiled. This might not work. But it might, and it was worth the try.

Before plugging in, she walked over to James. Linda was bent over her own computer, lost in her work. She was muttering to herself.

"James?"

He startled and looked down at her. "How are we getting out of here?"

Linn hadn't thought about it, but when she did, now, it was obvious. "Grandpa can open a portal in a building. I can't, I don't have the control to keep it where it needs to be. He'll get you out."

"What are we facing here? Angry mermaids?" He was smiling, but she saw the underlying concern.

Linn wasn't sure herself, but she had ideas. "They can do legs, you know. But I'm afraid they are just providing transport for goblins. The water folk rarely involve themselves directly, but they might have seen the return of Mac'Lir as a threat to their kingdom, with the power he has over the sea."

"I thought that was Poseidon?" James looked very confused.

"Only the Mediterranean and Red Sea." Linn felt frustrated. She didn't know what he knew, and didn't have time to tell him all of it. She'd had an intensive course for two years, but it still wasn't enough to have all the answers. She wasn't even sure her grandfather had all the answers. "The Atlantic belongs to Manannan Mac'Lir."

James still looked like she had hit him over the head with something heavy. "I knew my employers were powerful, but..."

"The fate of a world hangs on this mission." Linn looked up at him. "Just not necessarily our world."

He nodded, still looking stunned. "Well, that's good enough."

"What I came over to tell you, though, was that I'm going to activate that." Linn pointed at the arch.

"It's not already live?"

"On, but not on." Linn realized that wasn't clear. "I'm going to open the portal to another universe."

James gaped at her, and then waved a hand. "Oh, go right ahead. I mean, nothing else can surprise me at this point. Another world, sure, no problem. As long as it isn't Cthulhu...?"

He stopped with his eyebrows raised. Linn laughed and shook her head. "No, no... but there might be dragons."

"Really?!" James stopped. "Never mind, I don't want to know. Go do what you need to do."

Linn nodded and walked away. She liked the funny man, and watching his reactions had been a hoot. He was standing over Linda now, in what she could see was a guarding action.

Crouching by the laptop, Linn plugged the cable in. The keyboard lit up. She stared at it. That had never happened before. Maybe closing her eyes and letting the nanobots do the work would solve it, like it had before. She tried it... and was rewarded only by an angry buzz and warble that was definitely an error message.

She looked at the computer. It was the same as before, scrolling lines of code, endlessly cycling. Unlike the other time, this one didn't stop after a minute. Maybe she had to wait until it was finished. It was hard to wait while she knew the enemy was coming.

It was a race against time, and she sat and listened to the quiet. The room seemed even bigger with the mist gone, all the people gone, and only the faint clicks of Linda's computer to listen to. Linn sat on the cool floor, cross legged, and wondered if they would be able to activate the device. If not, then what? Just because she couldn't turn on, or off, the arch, didn't mean the goblins wouldn't.

She thought they would. Their ancestors had made it after all. Built to the dragon's specifications. For a second, she was angry at the coblyns for not coming here. It would have been so much easier with them doing this, rather than her and two humans who shouldn't even be here. What were they going to do after this mission? They wouldn't be allowed to return to a normal life, if they had one before.

She was put out with Quetzalcoatl, too. Mr. Q, really? Why hadn't he put immortals on this assignment? Linn closed her eyes and focused.

Being mad at everything and everyone wasn't going to help. She wasn't sure what she was doing, but she was sure that anger for things that happened long before she was born wasn't moving forward.

The laptop beeped, and her eyes flew open again. Was that hers, or Linda's? She looked down. Hers had stopped scrolling, and the blinking cursor flashed at the bottom of the screen. But Linda was standing up, now, and speaking.

"Dammit! It won't take the reprogram. I don't know what else..."

Linn closed her eyes, held her fingers over her keyboard, and let the power of Nyx flow through her.

Click.

Click.

Click.

2 2

MONSTER'S LOSS

*L*inn opened her eyes again. Nothing seemed to have happened. She looked at the symbols on the screen, but it wasn't blinking anymore. Linn looked across the mouth of the arch, at James and Linda.

Linda was staring into the arch. James stood behind her, his hand clenching like he was reaching for a weapon on his hip that wasn't there. Linn got up and moved around to see what they were looking at.

The arch had turned into an opening into blackness. There was nothing there. Something occurred to Linn. "This is the back."

They looked at her, startled by the sound of her voice. Linn walked around the arch, and they followed. On the other side, Linn had a little déjà vu. She had never seen this landscape, but she had seen it through Adel's eyes. She stared into the other world, swaying on her feet. The memories she'd shared made her want to step through, to call out to her lover, to...

Linn shook her head hard, and looked at her hand. She was clenching the little bone hard enough to hurt. Without thinking about it, she'd pulled it out of her pocket and was clutching it.

She was reminded that Linda and James existed when Linda walked up to the arch and put her hand into the other world.

"It tingles." The older woman had a dreamy tone, and an odd look on her face when she turned back to them.

James and Linn saw what was happening behind her. James started to leap toward his friend and partner, Linn stepped sideways to stop him, yelling.

"No! That's not an enemy..."

Linda spun around and saw the blue dragon. Linn didn't understand what she did next until much later in life. She was too young, had not spent a long life in pain and wanting to be someone, anyone, other than who she was. And she had never wanted to be a dragon. Linda went through the portal to Adel's world, where the ever-living had been changed from dragon to human facsimiles, and the little technicians had fled with enduring memories of slavery.

Linn would never know what Linda's fate was, but the look on her face as she ran to greet Ter'nian was ecstasy.

"Linda, wait!" Linn screamed, afraid to step through the portal. For a second, the adult woman stopped, looking back at the girl. Linn always wondered, after, if she thought they would try to force her to come back. Linn still had one arm in front of James' chest, but that wouldn't have stopped him, and he wasn't trying to move.

Linn hurled the bone through the arch. Linda put out her hands in a reflex, and caught it. It was perhaps baseball sized, and she juggled it, almost dropping it, in surprise.

"Give that to Ter'nian. It's very important." Linn spoke. Linda shook her head, and Linn shouted it as loudly as she could. Now Linda nodded. Behind her, the blue dragon was swooping in to a landing, and he was vast. The ground shook on that side of the portal when he landed. Linda turned to greet him, holding Adel's bone, with a kernel of his memories crystallized in it, cupped in her hands. The dragon circled his body around her, snaking his head around until he was peering through the arch, his vast eye all they could see.

He couldn't possibly fit through that. A nictating membrane closed over his eye, then opened again, a tear the size of Linn's head trickling from the corner of his eye.

Had they sent a child to guard the prisoners, because the adults were too big? Linn wondered. Or maybe Adel had been the equivalent of her age, when he was exiled. She knew it wasn't a full understanding, more like the glimmer of one.

They stared into his eye for a long moment. Linda was vanished from their sight, but slowly, Linn felt a voice form in her head.

"You are... a child."

"I am not only a child." Linn knew there was still growing, but after this... she wasn't a child.

"You know him."

Linn didn't have to ask what he meant. "I do. He can't return to you, and we wanted to warn you, before we closed the portal."

She felt James's twitch, beside her, and looked up at him. His face was twisted in something like pain. He twitched again.

"I speak to him. He is protector." The faint voice might have been deafening, were the portal not between her and Ter'nian.

"We fear for you." She informed the fantastic beast. It seemed like a foolish concern, looking at him now. But the goblins had seemed so rabid.

"I know." There was a sad flavor to the words. "We learned... and things are not as they were. We remain regretful, and it is not enough."

She got a gust of sensations. Pain, shame, guilt, and a peace with the system that had been developed in the turns of the galaxy since Adel had been locked away from him, by a treachery.

"We cannot allow this gate to remain." The voice was firm now, certain. Earth would have to make its own way, to create a harmony with the beings who all shared her surface and seas. "We will close it permanently. This... hooman, and I speaking to him."

"That's what we were trying to do." Linn shouted out loud.

James turned to her. "Run."

"What?" Linn blinked up at him. He looked funny, and not in a funny way.

The dragon's voice sounded in her head, "You will want to depart now, as your companion has asked my help to do something rather rash..."

"Run!" James repeated hoarsely, and pushed her, following her around the arch to the device. He stopped at it and started pressing buttons. He moved like a puppet on strings.

Linn ran. She was suddenly terrified. Linda was gone, looked happy. James was not James any more, she knew without needing to stick around to ask more questions. She wasn't possibly going to get out of Nyx before he set that thing off. It wasn't a full-yield nuclear device, it emitted a huge electromagnetic pulse, which should, in theory, kill any immortals within range by disrupting their nanobots and condemning them to a life of a mortal. It wasn't a fast death. She didn't want to live forever, but she didn't want to be close enough to find out what death by explosion or radiation felt like, either.

There was no one else in the room, just her own pounding feet. She wasn't going to make it... and she had an idea. Linn focused on the High Path, on forming a nice, small, portal to the other plane. It was hard, inside. They had been told not to do it, over and over, to only open one where they had room for error.

The patch of shimmering grey formed. It wasn't big enough. Linn didn't have time: there was a noise behind her, a flash that put a hard-edged shadow of her form into the High Path... she leaped, tucked, and rolled.

The floor of the tunnel wasn't soft, but she didn't lose any skin as she skidded into it, and scrambled to her feet, running to her grandfather, and hoping he had the boys with him. She had closed the Path before the second flash of the explosion, so she would live. Linn could feel herself shaking. She hadn't known the humans long, but they were both gone. Nyx was gone. Ter'nian had scared her on a level she didn't know existed.

What Linn really wanted was a hug, and a reassuring chat, and some hot cocoa.

What she found was a confused battle of sorts, and her grandfather with a look of distracted surprise. "Where the Hades..." He hacked offhandedly at a goblin, who was crawling across the scree with only one good arm. Linn looked away from what happened when half its head was gone.

She didn't get the hug. Instead, he produced a belt knife. "All I've got. Good you're alive. Watch out!"

Linn spun around and fended off the clutching hands of a dark naiad. She'd never seen one that color before. Seaweed green, blotchy, long sharp teeth, lots of them. And green blood, oozing slowly from her fingers where Linn had slashed them open.

Lambent had been a short sword, all Linn could handle. The knife wasn't much shorter than Lambent, but it was awkward. All she could do was be grateful the naiads didn't seem to have weapons beyond her taloned fingers and teeth. The fingers were on long arms, though, and the naiad was angry at Linn now.

Linn wasn't sure quite what to do. She hacked at the hands, and saw a finger come loose, flying off into the gravel beach.

"Grandpa!" She wailed. "How do you make these things stop?"

If she were properly armed, she wouldn't be this worried. She'd kill for a gun. This made her laugh, which startled the naiad out of her attack. She stared Linn in the eye. Linn lunged; knife gripped firmly.

Killing that naiad felt awful, and she was only going to have to do it again with a different one. Heff was fighting three goblins, Linn could see, and beyond him, Blackie and Merrick. The two were lined up head to tail, covering one another's backs. Other groups were scattered around within her sight – no one she recognized, but she decided that any naiads or goblins must be the enemy. The naiads had tridents, some of them. The long poles were intended for fishing and water use. On land they looked very awkward.

The goblins, on the other hand... some carried short swords, others knives. Her grandfather had left bodies in his wake, and Linn headed in that direction. She also wondered why the goblins didn't have guns, but she wasn't going to argue since she didn't have a gun.

The leaf-bladed sword she picked up was covered in gunk she didn't want to think about. Linn concentrated, hard, on it. "I'm naming you Nyx."

She could feel the blade take the power she was putting into it, and the gunk burned off. Linn didn't have time to contemplate that and why it didn't hurt. She ran toward Heff, holding the sword ready.

23

GOBLIN GUNK

*T*here was no cover. The doorway that opened to Nyx was a gaping hole, and everyone seemed to be avoiding it through some unspoken mutual agreement. The lip of the caldera wasn't any help. Linn wasn't sure just how live this volcano was, but she wasn't going to risk falling in it. The sea was still coughing up deep green naiads and their cargo of goblins on the shore. The circling seabirds overhead were expressing their displeasure in the only way remaining to them, which just made the loose stones underfoot even more slippery.

Each naiad carried one, sometimes two goblins. Linn wasn't sure how they were able to keep the goblins breathing, but she did know that her grandfather had spent his own boyhood under the sea, breathing. It was possible. It was also possible that the naiads were going to overwhelm the small force still on the island.

"Grandpa."

He turned a little, but didn't look fully at her. Linn was facing in the other direction, anyway. She'd cover one direction; he'd see the other. There was a lull in attackers, but she didn't know how long that would last.

"What, honey?" He sounded distracted, tired, and hoarse.

"Why don't we just let them pass?" Linn felt like her arms were broken.

She could hardly hold Nyx up. How long had they been fighting? Hours? Days?

"What happened down there?"

They hadn't had a chance to talk yet. Since Linn had dropped out of the High Path practically at his feet, they'd been only yards apart, but no time or breath to talk.

"The device was detonated." It wasn't time to talk about how, or by whom.

Grandpa didn't ask. "So, there is nothing down there."

"Only slow death." Linn wanted to lie down and sleep for... a long time. But not in a glass coffin. She shivered in the cold air, but she was sweating from effort.

"We can channel them into it. Go up to the rim." he ordered her.

Linn obeyed. Behind her, she could hear him roaring orders. Linn sat just below the rim, hugging her knees, still gripping Nyx in case a stray goblin popped up. Slowly, the people fighting broke free and retreated. At first, the goblins, angry and not too bright anyway, followed.

The naiads turned the tide. Screaming and hissing, they stormed toward the tunnel mouth. The goblins followed. By this time, Linn had Merrick on one side, Blackie on the other. They were both leaning on her, and she didn't mind that they were covered in nasty gunk. They were warm, and she was shaking.

They sat as the last of the goblins on the island ran into the tunnel.

"They'll come back out when they discover there is nothing left." Linn discovered her throat hurt. She must have been yelling again. She'd felt that way the last time, too.

Blackie licked her cheek.

"Ewwww..." Linn swiped at it with her free hand. "You don't know what's on me. Disgusting boy."

Merrick let his tongue loll out in a wolfish grin.

"We need to leave." Linn went on. She wasn't thinking fast, but she was thinking. If they simply walked away...

Grandpa Heff had the idea too, she saw. He opened and anchored a portal and was ushering people through as fast as they would move. Some couldn't move... she saw one man carry another through, slung over his shoulder. The dangling, bloody hand of the other man dragged on the rocks and Linn didn't think he was only unconscious.

She staggered to her feet and, weaving, headed for the portal. There would be another wave of attackers at any minute now, and she was just not moving fast enough. Linn was trying not to drag the tip of her sword in the rocks, but it was getting heavier with every step.

"Blackie, Merrick, in." Her grandfather pointed and they trotted through, looking like she felt. Every step was agony. Heff scooped her up, stepped into the portal, and close it behind them.

"Can you walk?" He asked her, putting her down. "We aren't going far."

"What about the naiads and goblins?" Linn had finally thought through what would happen next. She was trying not to think about what had come before.

"Mac'Lir is coming." He didn't say how he knew.

"I can walk." Linn put one foot in front of the other. "As long as it isn't far."

She was so glad to be off the island, to know she would never have to see that terrible place again, it gave her a second wind. She ached everywhere, but it was possible, she learned now, to keep going on for a surprisingly long time if one just put a foot down, and then another, a bit in front of the first one.

Linn knew Grandpa had said not far. She also knew Grandpa would have said anything to keep her moving. He was good at getting more out of people than they knew they had in them. She'd lost count of her steps, and the time, and even Blackie and Merrick, who were somewhere in front of her.

"Are we going to come out in Valhalla?" She asked blearily, addressing her grandfather's back as he walked in front of her.

He looked over his shoulder, "No, where did you get that idea?"

"It's where Loki was sending his people. And some of them are still with us."

Grandpa shook his head. "No, these are others. I think all the Norse had gone when the first wave hit the beach."

"Was that all of the goblins?" Linn remembered what Mac'Lir had said about an army.

"Probably not." Grandpa Heff dropped back a pace, next to her. "I know you are curious, but perhaps when we have gotten rest?"

Linn followed his point, and saw the end of the tunnel. They had arrived. "Oh, good."

She was the last person out of the portal, which faded into nothingness behind her. Linn stopped moving, which might have been a mistake, and looked around. She didn't recognize their surroundings.

"Where are we?"

When he had said not Valhalla, her next thought had been Mac'Lir's castle. It was close, geographically, to Iceland. Certainly, closer than the Sanctuary. Now, she was conscious that she was swaying on her feet, and standing in the midst of a perfect garden. The air was warm, gentle, and scented with flowers.

"Quetzalcoatl's Court." Heff took her arm, and she leaned a little on him. He had to be tired, too, but he felt solid and sturdy as they moved again.

"I don't want to be here." Linn wasn't thrilled with how slow her brain was. She didn't want to be here, her heart was sinking, and it took her until the turn in the garden path to remember why she had this dreadful feeling about being here, now.

"I needed to bring the lost ones, from Nyx, to him." Grandpa steered her toward a patio and a set of open French doors. Linn walked through the soft white curtains and balked.

"I'm muddy. And bloody." She was looking down at the beautiful rug. It was getting closer, slowly.

Over her head she could hear her grandfather calling for someone. The rug was soft on her cheek, and Linn closed her eyes, savoring the warmth, and the safety. Careful hands were picking her up, and she tried to open her eyes again, but they were so heavy.

Everything hurt, but that was getting further away now, too.

"She was injured recently, and hasn't given herself time to heal." Grandpa's voice, rough and exasperated. Linn tried to respond and point out that she had been doing important things.

"How bad?" Linn didn't know that voice.

Whatever the answer was, she didn't hear it. She was finally unconscious.

Linn woke up to the familiar smell of frangipani. She opened her eyes, looking for her grandmother, and then realized the scent was blowing in the open window. She sat up, and it was only then that she remembered she ought to hurt. She didn't hurt, but her mind was whirring like the hummingbird's wings.

The little bird darted into the room, and then back out again, looking for the flowers that were growing across the window and making the smell she had noticed. Linn stretched, swung her feet out of bed, and looked at her skin. She wasn't quite as blotchy as she had been. The feather on her palm was beginning to fade into an ashy grey rather than the stark black it had been when fresh. Her hair... that felt as though it were the same awkward cut as it had been. She wondered when she would have time to go see a stylist.

Right now, she had no time. She needed clothing, more than the thin nightgown she was wearing, and food... Linn put one hand on her stomach. Food, then to talk to people. Rather a lot of people, in places all over the world, and she wasn't looking forward to going anywhere. She wanted home, and to lie on the beach, and that was about it, for the foreseeable future.

The wardrobe yielded clothing in her size, if not her style. The long silk sundress was the closest to something she would consider wearing, everything else was lingerie, or evening wear. Linn contemplated the thought of jeans and a t-shirt wistfully. Hers had vanished, presumably for cleaning, if they weren't beyond repair. She seemed to recall various tears in cloth and clothing from the battle on the island. Battles were rough on clothes, and her body.

Linn did find that she was sore, and very stiff, as she moved around. Before dressing, she did some stretches and loosened muscles. There would be no threat here, with Quetzalcoatl and his people around, but she would rather be prepared. Food, then Grandpa, Blackie, and Merrick.

The hall was empty, and she hadn't been able to find shoes, besides high heels which were utterly out of the question, so she walked barefoot through the long hall and down the stairs, following her ears and smell to the big morning room. Small tables with chairs were scattered around this room, which was partly open to the outside, so you weren't quite sure if you were in the garden or the house, still.

Linn paused in the doorway, and then saw her goals. Blackie and Merrick, in boy form... no, men. She corrected herself, looking at them. They were focused on food and didn't see her until she was almost to them.

They had grown since this had all started. Merrick stood up when he spotted her.

"Linn." His face looked thinner than she remembered, and his hair was different.

Blackie leapt up, almost knocking his chair over, and hugged her tight. Linn gasped for air. He was solid, warm, and seemed to be healthy as a horse. She could hear his heart pounding against her cheek.

"Oof!" Linn gave him a squeeze, and then pushed away. "Gerroff me. I'm starved, and you just saw me last night."

She saw the look on their faces, and reached for a chair, sitting quickly before she met the floor up close again. "What is it?"

It was bad news, she could tell. Like when they had seen the damage from the troll's blood. The two of them were like glass, she could see right through them. "My mother? Deirdre?"

"Linn..." Merrick looked away, pressing his lips together, then back at her.

"Where is Grandpa?" Linn felt her voice go all squeaky the way it did when she was really upset. She hated it, but couldn't help it. "What's wrong?"

"No one's dead." Blackie took her hand, and shot a glare at Merrick. "It's not that."

"What is it, then?" Linn took a deep breath, relieved to hear at least that much.

"You..." Blackie cleared his throat, and looked at Merrick again.

Linn was beginning to feel irritated now. "Stop it, both of you. Just tell me."

"You've been asleep for a long time, Linn. You were really badly injured."

Now Merrick, of all people, was holding onto her other hand. Linn felt her fingers tremble as he cupped it gently, looking down at the pale skin in his own large, brown hand. Linn looked, too. The evenness of her skin made more sense, now, she had faded all over.

"I'm alive." She pointed out. "Was there any doubt?"

Merrick nodded. "They didn't know. It was a coma, your mom said. Internal damage, shock, I dunno what all. You made it here, and then collapsed entirely."

"Oh." Linn wasn't sure what to make of this. Blackie was squeezing the other hand tightly, and she didn't have the heart to tell him it hurt a little. "I feel okay right now?"

Merrick smiled. "I see that. You said you were hungry?"

Reminded, Linn's stomach growled. Merrick let go of her and got up. "I'll get Serafina."

Left alone, Linn looked at Blackie. "Where are..."

"Your mom is here, out in the gardens. Heff is off at Mac'Lir's quelling the last of the goblin offensives."

"Offensives?" Linn was even sure where to start asking questions. "Spot, Deirdre?"

"There's been several attacks. Dee won't leave the castle, says she is in no danger, and she didn't want to see you sick in bed, she'd wait until you walked through the library door."

Linn smiled. She could just imagine Dee refusing to accept she was dying. Linn still hadn't wrapped her head around that, either.

"Can you get Mom?" She asked Blackie, having decided that was the most important thing she wanted, out of everything in her brain at the moment.

He stood up, then bent over her, kissing her on the forehead. "I'm so glad..."

Blackie rushed away, but she had heard him get all choked up, and she sat staring into nothingness, wondering just how close she had been to dead and not sitting here in a delicate chair watching another hummingbird hover over a potted plant in full bloom.

Merrick returned with a tiny black-haired girl in tow. She was beaming, and carrying a tray of food.

"I wasn't sure what you'd want." Merrick explained. "This is Serafina."

"Hello." Linn was feeling rather detached and unreal. "Pleased to meet you."

"So glad to meet you." The other girl deftly slid plates and a glass of juice in front of her. "Call for me if you need anything."

Linn looked at Merrick. "I think I'm in shock."

"We didn't expect you to wake up. Eat..."

Linn nodded and obediently started on her breakfast, while Merrick kept talking.

"After... After we got here, it was chaos for a while. Quetzalcoatl was sorting out who the people from Nyx were, and where they should go. Your mother and grandmother arrived and stayed by your bedside for days. Mac'Lir sent word the goblins were descending on his castle yet again, and Q sent men to him. They asked if I would stay here, with you."

Linn sipped at her juice. Food was good, but she couldn't eat much. "Why?"

He squirmed a little. "Well, I wanted to stay. You might need me."

Linn tried to parse this into making any sense and failed. She went on to another topic. "And Nyx?"

"Last report I heard, dead as it is supposed to be. An overpass showed bones of all sorts being picked clean by seabirds. Even those will be gone soon, Q thinks. Heff said the nuke set off warning alarms, but Nyx dampened the effect, and it was written off by humans as volcanic activity."

Linn noted that Merrick was obviously more comfortable with Quetzalcoatl than she would ever be. Q?

It reminded her of something else. She was the only one who knew what had happened to the humans, in those last moments in Nyx. Which reminded her of the sword she'd had on the island. Had she dropped it?

Her mother's arrival distracted her. Linn stood and hugged her, both of them crying.

"I didn't mean to scare you." Linn told Theta, her voice wobbling.

"I know... Oh, baby." Theta held her tight for a long minute. Then she let go and wiped her eyes. "Sit, eat more. You have gotten so thin."

"I feel okay." Linn sat, though. She could eat more, now that she thought of it.

"I need to talk to Quetzalcoatl, Mom."

Blackie and her mother sat at the table, filling the available chairs.

"He will be back this afternoon," Theta frowned. "I want you to keep resting, Linn. No more adventures for a while, please?"

Linn shook her head. "No more for as long as I can get away with."

24

GLASS MAIDEN

*L*inn refused to return to bed for a nap after breakfast. "Mom, don't fuss over me. I think I've slept enough."

She did allow herself to be installed in a lounge chair on the broad patio, and to not talk about anything important again until Quetzalcoatl finally walked through the doors, wearing an elegant black suit, and paced toward her.

Linn sat up, but he waved her back. "Sit, child, and I will relax with you for a while. This peace is good after my journey."

He shrugged out of his suit coat and loosened his tie. Serafina appeared with icy glasses for both of them. Theta stood. "I will let you two talk. Q..."

"I know, my dear. I will not tire her out, nor cause her mental anguish."

He stood and hugged her mother, then watched her walk inside before turning back to Linn. He stood and looked at her, with both sights, Linn guessed, before sitting again.

"I know what you want to tell me about." He was sitting sideways on the lounger, leaning toward her with his elbow on his knees and hands loosely clasped in front of him. "You need not, if it will distress you. I can know, without the details."

"I need to." Linn did feel like she must talk it all out, but her throat was tight. She sipped at the fruity drink. "James is dead."

He nodded, a look of faint surprise on his face. "But not Linda?"

She shook her head. "I don't think so. She crossed over the portal, you see. I lost sight of her, but... I didn't feel like she was in danger. She seemed, I don't know, excited."

He looked thoughtful. "I can see that. Part of why she worked for me was that zest for the fantastic unknown she so longed for. It finally overwhelmed her common sense. I can only hope she never regrets that impulse."

"James was..." Linn remembered the puppet-like motions. "He detonated the device, when it couldn't be set off remotely."

"I presumed as much." Quetzalcoatl murmured. "Your grandfather told me the tunnel simply switched off, and he could feel the blast, but attenuated by the depth. It didn't affect his power. He was, I gather, shocked to think you had still been in the bowels of Nyx."

Linn remembered the look on Heff's face when she had fallen out of midair practically at his feet. "I really must learn to stop frightening my family."

The lean serpent god chuckled. "I am sure they would appreciate that. James did as he would have wanted, then, saving a world, and being a hero. Well, he would have hated that bit, but he was."

"He was a soldier?" Linn asked.

"Yes, he was. A staff sergeant, I believe, before a medical retirement and then I found his skills very useful."

"Did he have a family? Did Linda?" Linn had been worrying over that. Now, Quetzalcoatl shook his head.

"I hire those with very few connections to the human world. It makes things easier to manage."

Linn sighed. "He was nice. She was funny and kind."

"They were good people. We were privileged to know them."

Linn fell silent for a long moment, thinking. "What comes now?"

"Rest. You are healed, but it will take time to regain your energy, and this has changed you, Linnea, in ways you will not see, yourself. There will be times that you feel just as you were, and then in an instant it will all seem strange, and wrong. You can always talk to any of us."

Linn nodded. He stood up. "I won't tire you out, or your mother will be angry."

"I needed to make my report." Linn sat up. "I need to talk to Mac'Lir, too."

"There will be time for that, later. He is busy right now, and I will send him a message you are awake, at least. Rest."

He strode away into the house, and Linn lay back again. It was warm, sweet, and peaceful. That didn't banish the cold specters of the island, but it helped. She closed her eyes.

She didn't mean to go to sleep, but she had a feeling when she opened them that she had nodded off. Linn turned her head to see Blackie stretched out on the lounger next to her. He was reading a book with a lurid cover.

"What do you have?" Linn asked. He started at the sound of her voice, then turned the book toward her.

"Oh, I remember that author. Coyote likes him, and I read a bunch of his stuff. He doesn't finish series, though, you know?" Linn remembered vividly the first one she had read, with the nanotechnology like magic, and the fallen world when the tech was severely limited. It had given her the first clue to understanding Grandpa, and the old gods.

"Still fun to read, though." Blackie closed it.

"Was I asleep long?" Linn couldn't really tell. The climate here meant she might well have slept through another day.

"You're just in time for lunch." Blackie offered her a hand, and she got up slowly. Still stiff, but that was going to take time. She'd been in bed for months, and her muscles were shot.

"Sounds good. Stop treating me like I'm made of glass."

Blackie pulled his hands back from where he'd been hovering like he was going to carry her if she fell.

"I'm not," he denied.

"You are. I'm fine." Linn marched into the house and toward the big garden room where casual meals happened.

"Linn." Merrick waved them over. "I've just met..."

The other person at the table stood, and held out his hands for Linn. "Coyote." She said, hugging him. He smelled of woodsmoke and herbs and something undefinable. "You never travel this far!"

"Almost never." He corrected with a crooked smile. "I needed to see you."

"To see me?" Linn wondered why. It had to be Monster.

"We will talk after..." the food arrived, with Serafina and a silent man serving it.

"What happened at the Yellowstone Caldera?" Linn asked idly while they were eating. She knew her mother had been there, and then called away at least twice by her injuries. Coyote shrugged.

"It was tedious, but with us draining the power as fast as they could pump it in? The area is not going to erupt without help, and they meant to help it along."

Linn knew he meant the old gods, the Olympians. "Another defeat for them, then. Will they try again?"

Coyote looked grave. "We will see."

Once the meal was over, Coyote leaned across the table slightly. "You must come with me immediately."

"No." Linn didn't even think, it just popped out of her mouth. He shook his head.

"It's not a request. I need you."

Blackie growled a bit deep in his throat, and Merrick cleared his throat. Coyote looked at the boy.

"She said no." Merrick looked calm, which Linn found remarkable.

Linn sighed. "I can't. I can't talk to the Monster again."

Coyote nodded. "I know. But you have to. He doesn't want to see you, either."

"Then why?" Linn threw her hands up in the air, and stood up. "I'm not going."

She walked away, too upset to see where she was going, other than out into the garden. She hadn't seen her mother or Quetzalcoatl. Blackie and Merrick, she could feel them, were following her. Coyote stepped out onto the path in front of her, from a side path. Linn had no idea how he had gotten in front of her. She stopped, trying not to cry.

"I can't." She whispered.

Linn was thinking of James, his face blank, and the last words he'd screamed at her. Of his utter focus, and how it wasn't really him anymore. Ter'nian had done that, across worlds. What could Adel do? What had he done to her already?

"I can't go near him." Linn whispered.

"You won't be alone." Coyote held out his hand. She ignored it.

"Leave her alone." Merrick stepped forward, and put a hand on Linn's shoulder.

It steadied her, that contact, and she lifted her chin. Linn was remembering a staring contest with Loki, and how Merrick's grip had kept her from falling under the god's hypnosis.

Coyote stood like a statue, his face calm but his eyes pleading. Linn took a deep breath. "I need Merrick and Blackie, at least."

"Of course." Coyote didn't get a smug look, for which Linn was grateful. She really hated feeling like she was being manipulated.

"I can't leave without telling mother. Ade-" Linn caught herself. "He's thought I was dying for this long, unless he knew when I woke up?" She wasn't sure she wanted to hear the answer to that.

Coyote shook his head. "I would have brought you, slumbering like a princess in a fairy tale, for him to awaken."

"He's no Prince Charming." Linn was revolted. Merrick's fingers squeezed her shoulder as though he were unhappy, too.

"No, the fairy tales don't always get that right." Coyote lifted his gaze to Merrick's face, over her shoulder. "And she will be utterly safe, I assure you."

Linn turned away. "I must tell mother, and Quetzalcoatl, and get better clothing..." Her voice died in her throat. Her mother and Q were there, nodding. Either they had known, or Blackie had gone to get them while she and Coyote were talking.

"You need to go, I know," Theta said. She stepped forward and hugged her daughter, then looked at Coyote. "Be careful with her."

"You know I will be."

Q just nodded. "Linnea, Daughter of Fire..."

Linn felt that spark of irritation at that name, like she was some big damn hero or something. She was no hero.

He went on, oblivious of her reaction. "You are always welcome here. Be safe on your journeys."

Linn squeaked with alarm as they faded away, and she was looking at the familiar walls of a High Path. She spun around so fast she almost overbalanced, and Merrick caught her. Linn was angry at Coyote. "I'm barefoot!" She didn't quite yell.

"I'm sorry, but this is urgent." Coyote had Blackie in big cat form, leaning against him.

"Shoes!" Linn wriggled out of Merrick's arms. "And..."

They dropped a little, onto a familiar gritty surface. It was softer underfoot than Linn had expected, which was a small enough thing to be grateful for. She wouldn't have minded the barefoot as much, but months of being in bed had stripped away her Hawaii calluses. She was a tender foot.

Coyote was beckoning, and Merrick, with a sideways glance at Linn, walked toward him. She nodded at him. She was fine.

They left her alone. Linn stood in the ash, the wind swirling her skirt around her calves and her hair over her face. She was alone, and that wasn't right.

It crept in on her, the oddity of being here, and yet there was nothing. Everywhere else in the world this was right, and normal, and here... she had always felt the warm comfort of his mind, the humor glowing like a flame. It was cold, now. Linn closed her eyes.

"Monster?" She asked, reaching out with her power to find him.

There was nothing, not even an echo. Linn could feel her eyes prickle with tears. She opened them and wiped her eyes with the back of her hand, looking around. She was near the ribs, which were different than she had last seen them. The shaking of Monster's upset had sent them from neat, upright alignment to leaning every which way in drunken abandon. Linn walked through two of them, letting her fingers trail over the smooth, warm surface of the bone.

25

POINTY TAILED KITTEN

*T*here was a flicker, just a hint of a thought. Linn felt her heart thump, and her stomach turn over. She was terrified.

Linn leaned against the bone, wrapping her arms around it, leaning her cheek on the smooth surface. "I'm ready," she said.

She pictured everything in her mind, from shaking Linda's hand, to the hoarse shout of 'run' echoing in her ears. She could feel the tears rolling down her cheeks by the time she was done, and she wasn't sure if they were for her, the humans, or Adel.

The flicker came again, and then pulled away. "Wait." Linn asked. "Will you talk to me, please?"

Alone. The word echoed through her head, not a voice, but an emotion. Monster had finally accepted that there was no way to go home again. He was alone.

"You aren't dead." Linn insisted. "And I sent your bone to Ter'nian."

"You saw him?" The voice was little, unlike his usual presence. Linn pictured the vast dragon in her head again, focusing on making it as real for Monster as she could. Then she pictured the white bone arcing through the air, to Linda, and to Ter'nian.

"Why are you afraid?" He was coming closer; she could feel it. From wherever he had retreated to, far enough inside, away, hidden enough to frighten Coyote into coming for her.

"He was controlling James." Linn felt her damp face and her tight throat. The tears wouldn't stop, now they had started.

"No." Adel was there, now, the warm brown of his scales glinting in the sunlight. "He would not, could not, any more than I could."

"I–" Linn choked, unable to speak through the tears.

"James let him in, like you let me in." Monster was warm, wrapped around her, and petting her like a kitten. Linn felt a little hysterical giggle well up at that mental image.

"Then it was me." She hadn't been sure, all that mad journey back to Nyx, the fighting, the fleeing.

"You're a hero." Monster gave her an image of a tiny kitten, tail straight and bottled, pink mouth gaping in a hiss of defiance.

Now Linn did laugh. "No more heroic than that."

"Heroes don't try to be heroes. They just do, what needs to be done, whether it's convenient to them, or not."

Linn looked for someplace to sit. She felt woozy all of a sudden. "What comes after, Monster?"

"After what?" He helped her, as she sat on a vertebra, remembering the last time she'd used his bones for a chair.

"After growing up." Linn felt the warmth of the sun, just like last time. "After... adventures."

"You never stop growing, or learning. Remember?"

She did remember. The idea of the boys, and her, learning from Monster. And the concept that he never stopped growing, was mentally as vast as Ter'nian had been in physical form.

"You worried Coyote." Linn scolded him now. "And I didn't even have time to get shoes on."

"I'm apologizing to my friend now." Monster sounded unusually meek. "And I have asked Merrick Swiftfoot to bring you shoes."

Linn hadn't known Merrick's other name. "Thank you..."

She could see him, when she shaded her eyes with her hand, walking toward her, something in his hand. Linn waved. He waved back.

"The wolfling is strong and good." Monster sounded approving.

"He's my friend, nothing more." Linn hoped she'd put enough censure in her tone to keep the irrepressible being from teasing Merrick. Boys could be sensitive about these things.

"Are we all right?" She asked. She felt like they were, her whole body had relaxed when Monster had finally responded. "You aren't going to slink off and try to die?"

He laughed. Merrick grinned, holding out a pair of moccasins. "You might want these..."

"Want to stay here and go to college?" Linn blurted. He looked startled. She hadn't meant to say that all at once without working up to it. She wasn't sure how to take it back, though. "Um..."

"I took my GCSE's last spring." He helped her with the moccasins, kneeling in the ash. "I'd planned for University, and then Mac'Lir returned."

"Monster can teach us, and we can audit the MIT tech courses, and if between all of us we can learn fast enough, we'll be ready when the old gods try again." Linn explained rather breathlessly. She wasn't sure how much he knew about the old gods.

"Makes sense." He stood up, dusting off his hands, and cocked his head to one side, listening. "Monster says it would be nice to have company besides Coyote for a while."

Linn got up, and when Merrick offered an elbow to lean on, she took it. Being sick was the pits. "We will have to drag Dee away from her precious library, and make Spot show us his human side. And the woods here are great for a wolf to run around in."

Merrick stopped walking. She looked up at him. "What?"

"You don't mind?"

"The wolf thing?" Linn was confused. He nodded, with a shy expression. "My best friend is a big cat. Why would I mind?"

"I dunno." He started walking again. "It'd be good to get some time away from the fam."

"We'll have visitors, I'm sure, and Monster will let us have holidays, won't you?"

They both heard him that time. "Will you learn to treat me with respect?"

Linn got a mental image of a dragon in front of a vast whiteboard, wearing glasses, looking over the rims at her.

"No. And no adventures, either," she responded, mentally sticking her tongue out at him.

"You've earned that much, at least." Monster said. "With the portal and Nyx gone, it will be a long time before the peoples who share our worlds figure out what is next. They have been fixated on that... I have been looking only at that, for too long. Now, it's time to figure out how to get along without killing one another, or enslaving the humans. The humans are right on the brink, a little shove, and they will be able to take care of themselves."

Linn looked at Merrick. They were at the bottom of the stairs now. He nodded with understanding; Monster had spoken to both of them.

"Then we'll be a little shove. We can pass as human. Subvert and promote technology for all we're worth, once we've learned enough."

Monster, his voice impish as she reached out and touched the curve of his skull. "It will be magical."

Linn started to laugh out loud. She might have nightmares, in the time to come, but she would never forget how to laugh.

WHAT COMES NEXT?

When I started writing Vulcan's Kittens I was just learning. It was only the second novel I'd ever attempted, and the first one I'd completed. It took me a long time to be ready to come back to Linnea and Heff's world, and attempting to write a convincing teenaged boy in the shape of Merrick was daunting. Before I could do it, I had to write Pixie Noir and Trickster Noir, but the fans of Vulcan's Kittens were still asking what had become of Linn and the kittens, and the weapon she helped build. I hope you enjoyed this book.

I did decide to end Linn's story here, for now. I'm not going to say I will never come back to it, but she's very grown-up and independent. I'd planned for that to be all, of the Children of Myth, but then... I was talking to my friend Peter Grant, who has written the Steve Maxwell science fiction series. He's from South Africa, and was telling me about African myths. Later, talking to my Evil Muse, he told me I should write Deirdre's story, and Spot, the enigmatic cat. Inspiration struck, and I will write her tale sometime soon. But I have other things to do first, so you shall have to be patient, and perhaps remind me from time to time...

AUTHOR BIO

Cedar Sanderson is a writer, blogger, and businesswoman who can be found in her office pounding the keyboard when she isn't out walking the dog. Her work has been published by Stonycroft Publishing, Naked Reader Press, and Something Wicked. She is the author of the young adult novel Vulcan's Kittens, and her second novel, Pixie Noir, will be released late 2013. She writes regular blog columns at Mad Genius Club, in addition to her own writing blog, where she posts almost daily. She prefers science fiction, mostly writes fantasy, and dabbles in non-fiction when her passion is stirred.

OTHER TITLES BY AUTHOR

Short Stories and Novellas

Voyageur's Cap (Published by Naked Reader Press) - Space Pirates and the return of the Hudson's Bay Company.

Memories of the Abyss - She may be crazy, but she knows her only friend was murdered.

Stargazer - Science fiction short story of a mother's love.

The Twisted Breath of God - A story of second contact with aliens.

Little Red-Hood and the Wolf-Man - Who's afraid of the big bad wolf? Not little Red with her shotgun!

Dwarf's Dryad - Who rescues whom from the Witch and her rapunzel?

Plant Life - Exploration of a new planet and first contact.

Snow Angel - A mother's love can defy any power, even that of angels.

Sugar Skull - what would you do to keep your job?

Novels

Pixie Noir- book one in the Pixie for Hire series. Lom must bring Bella Underhill. Nothing personal, it's just his job.

Trickster Noir - Book two of Pixie for Hire. Lom is broken, perhaps dying, and Bella must take up the job of being Underhill's enforcer. Together they will face their worst fears and greatest joys.

Vulcan's Kittens - Vulcan's granddaughter is kitten-sitting when an old war comes to them. She must protect them at all costs, because they aren't just kittens.

The Eternity Symbiote - the aliens came in peace, bearing gifts. What could go wrong?